LORRAINE WILSON

I live in Wiltshire with my husband but love to travel and have lived in four continents. From playing amidst Roman ruins in Africa as a child to riding a Sultan's racehorse in the Middle East as a teen, I've many experiences to draw on for the stories I've been writing ever since I can remember. When I'm not writing you'll find me listening to audiobooks while I sew or design handbags, usually with a rescue terrier or two curled up on my feet!

www.facebook.com/LorraineWilsonWriter

@Romanceminx

Rebellion of a Chalet Girl

LORRAINE WILSON

Harper*Impulse* an imprint of
HarperCollins*Publishers* Ltd
1 London Bridge Street
London SE1 9GF

www.harpercollins.co.uk

A Paperback Original 2015

First published in Great Britain in ebook format by Harper*Impulse* 2015

A catalogue record for this book is
available from the British Library

ISBN: 9780008142551

Automatically produced by Atomik ePublisher from Easypress

In memory of Celia Cady, 'mother' and lifeline to many.

Also special thanks to both the lovely team at Harper Impulse and to Catherine and Dawn for everything.

Chapter 1

Okay, Tash got it. There were some very important people coming to stay at Chalet Repos.

Blah-de-blah.

Did they really need yet another 'briefing' from Holly? And since when had she taken to scheduling briefings into the day anyway? You cleaned, you cooked and you were always polite to the guests. Even when they really, really hacked you off and you were hung-over. There wasn't much more to it, surely?

Tash could do this job in her sleep. Sometimes it felt like she almost did.

She nestled back into the comfy brown leather sofa and yawned. It'd been a late one last night and even once she'd got to bed she hadn't slept much. But then she caught Holly's gimlet eye and shrugged sheepishly in reply.

"So, you all get how important this is, right?" Holly asked, perched on the edge of an armchair covered with a faux fur throw, one hand resting lightly on her barely visible bump.

Everything's changing around here. Holly's pregnant, Sophie's moved out and engaged. And now we're having 'briefings.' Not to mention the rumours about the other changes that might be coming.

A wave of panic swelled in her chest, threatening to submerge her. Why couldn't things stay the same?

Tash's gaze fell on Rebecca, Sophie's replacement. Rebecca's high blonde ponytail bobbed up and down as she nodded earnestly at Holly, bright lipsticked smile in place. Amelia and Lucy also appeared bright-eyed, if not quite so bushy-tailed. Tash glanced back at Rebecca's hair. You didn't get hair that sleek and bouncy using supermarket's own-brand shampoo and dying it yourself over the bathroom sink.

Tash examined one of her own split ends with a sigh. She didn't give a flying snow fairy what anyone thought about the home-dyed pink stripes on her mousy hair but it might be nice to get her hair done properly one day. If she could ever afford it.

"Tash?" Holly asked, eyebrows raised, a mixture of impatience and concern in her eyes.

"Um, no, not so much..." Tash admitted. "Aren't all our clients important? And I think we're pretty nice to them already. Just how extra nice do you want us to be exactly?"

She smirked and Amelia and Lucy sniggered. Only Rebecca remained straight-faced, hands folded primly on her lap.

Maybe the rich pay to have their sense of humour surgically removed too?

Holly rolled her eyes. "Not *that* nice obviously. Weren't you listening to anything Tash?"

Maybe she should plead this morning's hangover in her defence? On balance, probably not. Now Holly was pregnant and not drinking, her sympathy quota for hangover symptoms had been drastically reduced.

"I'm sorry, I got a bit distracted." Tash met Holly's stare. "I'm listening now."

They both knew she'd been tuning out a lot lately. Not to mention getting drunk as often as she could afford to. Mind you that was kind of tuning out on a bigger scale if you thought about it, something she tried very hard not to do. It wasn't illegal and was a hell of a lot safer than some of her other coping mechanisms.

Anyway this job was a doddle.

Until Holly had decided to rewrite the job description, that was.

"Hmm, I'll be testing you at the end." Holly raised her eyebrows a fraction.

Is she going to ask me to stay behind at the end? Put me in detention?

Tash suppressed a sigh; that thought wasn't fair. She owed so much to Scott and Holly. They'd been good to her. More than good, they were almost like family. As one of the longest standing chalet girls at Chalet Repos and the only one who got to stay all year round, Tash already got a lot of slack.

She'd never actually told Holly all the gory details about her past and growing up in care but Holly seemed to know she'd had a lot of serious crap to deal with. In her bleaker moments, Tash glimpsed an empathy in Holly's expression, a recognition and understanding of pain. Sometimes the weight of all the unspoken memories threatened to cave in on Tash but still she couldn't, wouldn't verbalise them. Where on earth would she start?

And what would be the point?

But the knowing light in Holly's eyes when they talked was a comfort. Maybe it was an understanding that came from having her own crappy family history to deal with. Holly and Scott knew Tash had nowhere else to go, no family to go home to and they'd kept her on to help with the cycling and hiking tours in the summer, taking care of her work permit. Not that they'd really seemed to need the help initially, but apparently that was about to change.

Everything was.

She stared across at Holly's small bump. It was ridiculous really, almost like she was feeling the insecurities of a toddler jealous of a new sibling but...well it was kind of how she felt. A part of how she felt at least.

Though she'd sooner die than admit it.

Amelia said she'd overheard them talking about expanding and discussing moving out of Chalet Repos when the baby was born so their room could be used as another guest room and they could have more space elsewhere. More privacy.

Where does that leave me?

"I'll give you the condensed version." Holly absent-mindedly stroked her bump, patting the fabric of her lime green hoodie. The colour contrasted well with her auburn hair. "These clients will have exclusive access to Chalet Repos for the whole of March. Although they may fly back to London a couple of times during that period and they'll also need shuttling to and from Geneva for meetings. They want to know *everything* about how we operate, the experience days we offer, what we feed our guests...everything. If they like what they see...well, this could be big for us. Really huge."

Holly's imploring gaze rested on Tash.

Because if anyone stuffs it up for them it's going to be me? Thanks Holly.

Tash stared down at the tan and white cow skin rug at her feet. Okay, so there'd been a few incidents the first season she'd been with Scott and Holly. When balding men with large beer guts and even larger egos made lewd remarks or tried to grope her bum like she was part of the services Chalet Repos offered, well it flicked a switch in her and she lost it. But still, she'd got a lot better about controlling her temper and it was hurtful they thought she'd do anything to screw this up for them.

"Don't worry, I'm sure you can trust us all not to mess up," Tash replied, swallowing down the hurt and meeting Holly's gaze again.

"Great." Holly smiled but a small crease in her forehead betrayed her persistent concern. "So if anyone in the group, you know, tries it on, just politely decline and come and tell me. Then I'll get Scott to have a firm but discreet word. But really, I can't imagine we'll have any of those sorts of problems. We're talking about a group of business professionals after all, not a stag do."

Tash snorted, looking sideways at Amelia. "I didn't hear anyone complaining about the last stag do group we had staying here!"

Amelia flushed pink but smiled. "Okay, you may have a point. I'd say Amy seems pretty happy with Josh. Did you hear about

4

that Rebecca?"

"The chalet girl who ran off with the bridegroom staying here at Chalet Repos?" Rebecca asked. "Yes, Tash told me. And she mentioned that your boyfriend Matt was part of the same group."

"Well, Josh was Amy's ex," Amelia said. "And as for Matt and I, well...I wasn't going to say anything until we'd chosen the ring but...we're getting married. This is going to be my last season as a seasonnaire."

Amelia's smile became a smug 'I've snagged my man' grin.

Oh fantastic. Another one.

Tash ignored the savage twist in her gut and forced a smile to her lips. "That's great Amelia, congratulations."

Holly, Lucy and Rebecca dutifully exclaimed, squealed and crowded round to hug Amelia. Tash tried to get her emotions under control, focusing on a snagged nail on her little finger.

Everyone else is moving on...

"Well Matt was fantastic when mum was sick last year." Amelia smiled contentedly. "And he persuaded me I couldn't be a seasonnaire forever. I mean, it's been fun but it's time to grow up, you know?"

"Right," Rebecca said, nodding seriously, as though Amelia were dispensing pearls of wisdom instead of a baseless platitude.

Tash stared out through the plate glass window. The falling snow swirled, buffeted by strong gusts of wind. She couldn't shake a sense of unease so visceral it twisted again at her gut, sending anxiety coursing through her veins.

Why does everything have to change? Everything was fine as it was.

Holly disentangled herself from the others and made her way over to Tash. She sank down on the sofa next to her.

"Actually Tash, there's something else I needed to tell you." Holly laid a hand on Tash's arm, her diamond engagement ring and platinum wedding band prominent on her wedding finger. "I thought you and Rebecca could accompany the group on a couple of their experience days and generally show them around Verbier?

You know, take them to places like the W. Make sure they have a really good time. Impress the pants off them."

Tash raised an eyebrow. Holly giggled and Tash couldn't help laughing too, even though she really didn't feel like it.

Holly's eyes lost their anxious expression, her face transformed by a relaxed smile. "Bad choice of words. I'd do it myself but I get so tired in the evenings at the moment and some days the so-called morning sickness lasts all day. I don't think throwing up on my shoes and then going to bed at nine o'clock would impress them much. You don't mind, do you?"

Tash hesitated. If only Holly had picked Amelia or Lucy instead of Rebecca to go along with her. But this was how Holly worked. Subtle, thoughtful and always working to keep the peace.

Holly's picked Rebecca because she hopes it will mean the two of us will finally start to get along.

She met Holly's eyes and was surprised to see a genuine concern for Tash's approval.

Doesn't she know by now I'd do pretty much anything for her?

After all Tash could count on one hand the number of people she truly trusted, and have fingers left over.

Scary thought that the two people I care most about in the world are moving on without me.

"Of course I don't mind, it'll be fun." Tash smiled. "Stop worrying, it'll all work out fine and I'll help out any way I can."

It was time to step up.

It scared her, becoming needed, relied upon. Needing... It was bloody terrifying.

Maybe she should've moved on years ago, before she'd had time to grow close to anyone. After all she'd been at Chalet Repos longer than she'd stayed in any one place before. The longest settled spell in her entire life in fact.

Stop it Tash, no looking back remember? Thinking about anything too much is dangerous.

Holly disappeared down the corridor to the office, to the desk that stood back to back with Scott's. What must it be like to find someone you loved so much you could actually live and work with them and not want to kill them?

Anxiety made Tash jittery and she tugged again at her snagged nail, breaking it off far too low but not caring that it hurt. The blurring of the line between emotional and physical pain was dangerous. Not that this really counted but she could imagine what the official line would be. That it was the thin edge of a very dangerous wedge.

She was done with that, with the old Tash.

But boy was it tempting sometimes.

I need caffeine. Caffeine and some ibuprofen.

Maybe it wasn't a good idea when she was anxious but she needed...something and really, how harmful could one cup of coffee be?

"So girls, what do we think?" Lucy's bird like eyes gleamed. She'd tucked her feet beneath her on the armchair so she looked tinier than ever, dwarfed by an oversized rusty-red cable knit jumper pulled down to her knees over her leggings.

"What do we think about what?" Tash replied, resting her head back against the sofa and crossing her arms over her chest. "Are we talking about the engagement epidemic or the fresh new talent about to hit Chalet Repos? Sorry to disappoint you hun but a group of suits are not going to satisfy your heart's wicked desires."

"Who says they're wicked?" Lucy quipped. "Don't judge us all by your own standards. Some of us are actually looking for a meaningful relationship with a grown up."

Ouch.

Tash laughed to conceal the sting, fingers curling into her palms beneath her elbows, nails pressing hard against her skin. Lucy was only joking, but...

"I think it sounds really exciting. Do we know anything about them? Maybe it'll be someone famous if they're so important." Rebecca sighed, her pale blue eyes becoming dreamy. She crossed her legs demurely, back still ramrod straight like she'd been taught to sit like that at finishing school or Cheltenham Ladies College or whatever Sloanesville academy she'd sprung from.

Tash's jaw clenched instinctively, like it did pretty much every time Rebecca spoke.

God I miss Sophie.

"It won't be anyone famous." Tash rolled her eyes. "How many famous investors do you know? It'll be another group of poncy businessmen in fancy Saville Row suits and handmade shoes they can't get wet in the snow. They'll expect us to jump every time they click their fingers. If they can prise their fingers away from their BlackBerries that is."

"Now, that's where you're wrong," Amelia said, a slow smug smile creeping across her face. "The name the chalet is booked under is Nathaniel Campbell. I checked the bookings spreadsheet and then I googled him."

She paused, relishing the fact she'd got everyone's attention.

"Go on." Lucy nudged Amelia with her elbow. "Don't leave us hanging. You have been watching way too many elimination shows. It doesn't create tension, it's just annoying."

"It turns out Nathaniel Campbell is on that programme *In the Lion's Den*. You know, the one where anyone under twenty-five with a business plan can go to beg for grants or internships. He's forty-eighth on the Sunday Times Rich List too; his specialty is buying companies with potential, turning them around, then selling them on again." Amelia grinned, eyes gleaming.

"You already have a fiancé, remember." Tash said quickly.

Sophie must've rubbed off on me. Who would've guessed I'd be the one taking the moral high ground?

But with Sophie gone someone had to do it. The gap Sophie had left when she moved in with Luc felt immense. And Rebecca certainly wasn't the girl to replace her. There was nothing immediately obvious to explain why, but it'd been apparent within days that Tash and Rebecca weren't going to be the best of friends.

8

Well nothing obvious except for the huge gulf between their backgrounds. Tash *had* tried.

Sort of.

"I've seen *The Lion's Den*," Rebecca beamed like she'd just won the lottery. "I love that programme. Nathaniel Campbell is seriously hot. He's the sexiest Lion on the show."

"I haven't seen it. Have you Tash?" Lucy asked.

"No." Tash shrugged and got off the sofa.

But then I haven't been back to England since I was eighteen.

"How do you know it's *the* Nathaniel Campbell?" Tash stopped at the doorway and turned back towards Amelia.

"How many Nathaniel Campbells do you think there are with the kind of money you need to invest in Verbier property?" Amelia asked. "Anyway I found his most recent interview online and when asked about new projects he said he was taking some time out in the Swiss Alps to write a companion book for the series. That would explain why he's booked Chalet Repos for the whole month."

"Hmm. I need a caffeine fix." Tash shrugged. "Coffee anyone?"

It was irrational to dislike a man she'd never met but telling herself so didn't stop the stirrings of resentment.

Nathaniel Campbell was bringing change to Chalet Repos and that was a good enough reason for Tash.

"I've seen him, I've seen him," Rebecca squeaked, practically bouncing up and down with excitement. Gone were her casual clothes, replaced by smart black wool trousers and a gorgeous aquamarine cashmere sweater. She even wore her tiny pearl earrings and a Tiffany pendant.

Her clothes whispered wealth and style.

"Great," Tash replied without enthusiasm as she pulled a clean navy hoodie on over her vest top, her sole concession to dressing up for the guests. She might not have been so irritated if Rebecca hadn't spent most of the previous evening talking about what she should wear and what Nathaniel Campbell would be like in real life.

Tash's mix of charity shop and cheap supermarket clothes felt like rags compared to the designer cashmere clothes Rebecca wore.

I feel cheap. In pretty much every sense of the word.

She wondered for the umpteenth time if she could last the whole season without cracking and pushing Rebecca down a black ski run.

Minus the skis.

It wasn't as if Rebecca even had to work, her father was a judge, they were minted. She even had a pony back home in Surrey for frick's sake.

Something tightened in her chest at the thought of it. A proper home. A safety net. Rebecca had it with bells on and Tash...didn't. Not that she expected life to be fair; she'd given up that hope long ago.

The familiar tension crept into Tash's jaw as she applied her eye shadow. Rebecca was doing the 'chalet girl thing' for fun because 'Daddy says I need to get a job. It's like, character forming, you know.'

Tash stared at Rebecca now in much the same way as she'd stared at her when she'd explained why she was at Chalet Repos, as though Rebecca had flown in from another planet, another universe even. It often felt like they spoke a different language.

"Do you really think some business mogul come TV star is going to take up with a poxy chalet girl?" Tash shook her head.

"Maybe." Rebecca grinned.

Tash tutted. "You have been watching too many romantic comedies."

There was a certain childishness to Rebecca's expression, a naïvety that stirred an unexpected protectiveness in Tash. She felt twenty years older than her, not the mere two years older she actually was. Rebecca was twenty-one but she seemed far younger than Tash had been at her age.

From what Tash had gleaned, Rebecca had seen practically nothing of the world outside her Surrey pony club idyll, private school and holiday villas in Tuscany.

She didn't seem to have a clue just how cruel human beings could be to each other.

Lucky her. Yet the lack of knowledge made her so vulnerable.

How can I hate Rebecca one minute and want to protect her the next?

Tash sighed. This was what dormitory living could do to you. Just the way someone else was breathing or humming along to their iPods could be enough to wind you up after two months of forced proximity.

Mountain Cabin Fever, Holly called it.

Rebecca rummaged in her make up bag for lipstick and applied it. When she smiled at Tash there was a pink smear on her front teeth.

"Wait." Tash touched Rebecca's arm, the cashmere super-soft beneath her fingertips. "You've got lipstick on your teeth."

It's not Rebecca's fault she isn't Sophie.

"Oh, have I? Thanks." Rebecca pulled out her compact mirror and a face wipe to remove the smear.

"Where are Amelia and Lucy?" Tash asked, making her way to the door.

"Already out there." Rebecca pushed her make-up bag beneath her bunk. "Wait for me."

Tash rolled her eyes as she waited, but not so as Rebecca could see. Tash wasn't a total bitch. Being friends with Sophie and Holly seemed to have sandpapered away some of her sharper edges.

But prickles aren't all bad. They keep you safe; just ask a hedgehog.

Had staying in one place for so long turned her soft?

In Chalet Repos' living area Amelia and Lucy handed flutes of champagne to men wearing dark suits and expensive leather shoes. Champagne at eleven in the morning? These guests must be considered important. But suits in a ski resort? Looked like she'd been right. There were four in the group, all with their backs to her. On closer inspection one of them turned out to be a woman

11

in an androgynous trouser suit and a very short pixie haircut.

Tash lingered by the doorway, feeling out of place. Rebecca edged forward, fixed smile in place, trying to make her way to the front of the group. Tash cringed for her.

Could she be more obvious?

Tash decided to skulk at the back of the room, straightening a few faux-fur cushions on the sofas and hoping to be left alone if she looked busy. Delaying the inevitable and much dreaded small talk she'd doubtless have to engage in.

When the cushions were plumped and the throws straightened Tash headed to the fireplace and threw another fresh log on the fire, even though it didn't really need it.

She scanned the room for any other unnecessary jobs and met Holly's eye.

"Tash," Holly called out. "Come over here and meet Mr Campbell."

Chapter 2

Why did you have to choose me to babysit this guy? I'm no good at this. No good at...suits. Give me a bar or a club and I can talk for England but not this...

The summons gave Tash no choice but to move reluctantly forward.

He's only a man.

Just a man.

Holly met her halfway and linked her arm through Tash's, as though afraid she was planning to leg it. Tash held her head high. No twat in a suit would intimidate her. Weren't you supposed to imagine people naked to make it easier?

Her stomach twisted over and her muscles tensed. Suits reminded her of officialdom, of all the adults who'd moved her around foster placements, who'd laid down the law and made decisions about her life without consulting her.

"Mr Campbell, this is Natasha...er, I mean Tash." Holly cleared her throat. Her nervousness somehow transmitted directly to Tash's stomach. "She'll be showing you round Verbier and getting you up to speed on all the experiences we offer guests."

Then Holly half shoved Tash towards the tall guy standing nearest them.

Tash looked up, forcing herself to look him directly in the eyes, annoyed by the nerves coursing through her body and determined not to show them.

Remember he's no better than you, just because he's wearing an expensive suit.

She'd expected a plastic man with an inflated ego and a TV tango tan but Nathaniel Campbell couldn't have been further from her imaginings. He had rugged features and was tall, powerfully built, like he'd been designed for the rugby field or maybe even a boxing ring, not an office.

There was a sharp intelligence shining in his flinty blue-grey eyes. A spark of desire tinged with fear sent a shiver of electricity the length of Tash's spine. She'd need to watch her step with this one.

He's nobody's fool.

Suddenly imagining him naked became a much more interesting proposition.

And it did nothing to relax her.

Worse still, as he focused all his attention on her it felt like he might be imagining her naked too.

He had an aura of power, a supreme confidence that Tash had been trying to fake her whole life. The difference was Nathaniel Campbell wasn't faking anything.

Stop acting like a crazed fan and act normal for frick's sake.

"Pleased to meet you." Tash held out her hand, pleased she'd finally remembered how to speak and co-ordinate her limbs. "By the way, nobody calls me Natasha, I'm Tash."

Amusement glinted in his eyes as he took her hand and shook it with a firm grip. Her hand looked tiny in his; she couldn't help staring at his hands. She'd experienced instant sexual attraction before but this was crazy.

Crazy stupid but sort of crazy good too.

It felt like the air had been squeezed out of her lungs. Electricity buzzed through her again but this time it was more of a shudder than a shiver. It felt, bizarrely, like there was no one else in the room. No one who mattered anyway.

It must be his famous charisma.

I'm as bad as Rebecca, I need to get a grip.

"Well lots of people call me Mr Campbell, or Nathaniel, but I prefer to be called Nate." His mouth twitched at the corners into an almost smile.

"And of course we have Mr Campbell's team - Mr Benson, Mr Smith and Ms Miller." Holly gestured to the rest of the group, her cheeks flushing pink as she sipped at her orange juice.

This isn't easy for Holly either.

"Please do call me Nate, we don't need to be formal." Nate turned and smiled at Holly. She received the full wattage of his smile and a pang of jealousy pierced Tash.

Watch it, you'll be acting as bonkers as Rebecca if you're not careful.

Yet on closer inspection his smile was that of a politician's; while genuinely warm and conveying that the recipient was the most important person in the room, there was a detachment in his eyes.

"And you must meet Rebecca." Scott stepped forward, resting one proprietorial hand on Holly's shoulder and gesturing to Rebecca with the other.

Rebecca shot forward eagerly, a pearly pink smile stretching widely across her face. She actually giggled when Nate took her hand.

Tash bit her lip. This was stupid. It wasn't like getting laid was a problem for her. Sex was...just sex. An urge, a bartering tool, an itch to scratch... She didn't need to get to know this man, there were plenty of others out there.

Ones who don't come with a health warning - Caution, this man could seriously affect your ability to string a sentence together and keep your pants on!

Hormones might be trying to hijack her body but she refused to act like a bitch on heat.

"I believe you know my father? Justice Crawley?" Rebecca simpered. "I'm sure he mentioned he met you at a political fundraiser."

Of course he did.

Tash resented Rebecca's instant elevation to the 'one of us club' just because of an accident of birth. It happened all the time in the Verbier trustafarian set. If a social connection could be established, if you'd been to the right school or knew someone in common, then you ceased to be 'below stairs.'

Ridiculous.

Even if I could afford the expensive clothes I'd still never fit in.

It was like they were still in the Middle Ages. How could anyone in the twenty-first century still believe birth into a certain class determined your worth?

It made Tash want to do very bad things.

"I believe I may have met Justice Crawley, yes." Nate replied gravely.

Yeah right, clever answer. Like he has a clue who Rebecca's talking about.

She narrowed her eyes at him and as though he sensed her looking he turned and met her gaze. A sharp jolt of connection surprised and thrilled her. A current passed between them, Nate's look so arrogant and knowing it made her insides squirm. When he looked away again she felt simultaneously relieved and disappointed.

Get a grip girl.

She'd never watched *The Lion's Den*. Surely anyone who wanted to be on TV had to have an ego the size of a planet? Yet, much as she wanted to, she couldn't dismiss him. He didn't suit the label she'd written for him.

Heart pounding, she stood back from the group, sipping at the flute of champagne Scott had handed her, bubbles dancing on her tongue. The champagne was expensive. Gaining favour obviously really mattered to Holly and Scott.

She could do this - be polite, show them around, be professional and not kill Rebecca in the process...

She stared at Rebecca who smiled coyly at Nate while touching him oh so casually on the arm.

Really? Maybe I'll have to revisit that 'not killing' part.

Tash snorted, quietly she'd thought, but Nate looked up and met her gaze from across the room, his stare piercing. Was there a flicker of understanding there? A shared joke or connection? Before she could decipher the look he turned back to Rebecca, listening politely to her chatter as though he'd never looked away.

Tash backed into a corner and decided to eat as many nibbles as she could; she'd felt too rough this morning to eat any breakfast. Best leave the boring small talk to the others. They were so much better at it than her and she was going to have to work up to a full on tour guide act. She couldn't do it cold. Who knew what might come out of her mouth at the moment?

Leaning against the back of a sofa she retreated into the unfocused, barely there look she'd perfected over the years to stop morons approaching her. She felt Nate's presence next to her before she saw him, felt the embarrassing jerk of her body's reaction to the warmth of him.

She turned to face him. It was always better to face matters head on, to take control of situations, relationships, pretty much anything really. Better to be the one who acted than sitting around waiting for others to do things to you.

"So, Holly tells me I'm going to be your guide for Verbier?" She said the only thing that came to mind while trying to solve the problem of where to look. Looking directly into his eyes, while kind of thrilling, felt dangerous. Like she might turn into Rebecca and involuntarily start touching him or something.

Ick. I refuse to turn into a sappy girl.

She settled for looking just past him, as though scanning the room. Then she realised how rude that was and reluctantly turned back to staring at the cool eyes assessing her and the thick eyebrows quirked into a question.

It felt intense, intimate.

Just a step away from a kiss...

"You don't want to ask me if I'm a keen snowboarder or if I've been to Verbier before?" His lips twitched into an almost smile. "They seem to be popular questions today."

"No." Tash returned the half smile, tentatively. Whatever *this* was, this *thing* happening to her, she was losing control of it rapidly.

Her heart pounded and she folded her arms across her chest, hugging her body.

Because if I'm holding myself my fingers can't stray to his arm to feel the muscles beneath that expensive suit. This is crazy. It's just sexual attraction. It means precisely nothing.

"Thank God, I hate wasting time on small talk." Nate exhaled and appeared to relax. It was a compliment, this assumption of a shared attitude. Heat crept up Tash's neck.

He's a suit Tash. Don't fall for the charm. You and Nathaniel Campbell have nothing in common.

"Because time is money?" Tash couldn't help the hint of snark in her tone; it escaped before she could suppress it.

"No," he replied, expression unchanging, seemingly unbothered by the jibe. "Because bullshit bores me and I've got better things to do with my time. But sometimes needs must."

"I suppose so," Tash replied doubtfully.

If you want to take on world media domination that is. First a TV show and now a book? Working in television must involve a lot of bullshit.

Nate's mouth widened into a wide smile, as though he'd heard her thoughts and found her beyond funny. A warm glow radiated through Tash.

How annoying to be so easily manipulated by the twitch of a few facial muscles. Get over yourself Tash.

"Could you show me my bedroom?" Nate asked.

Heat spread from her neck to her cheeks.

I'm blushing now?

Tash cringed. She was blushing like a teenager. And she'd never even blushed when she actually was a teenager!

It's a simple request, not a come on, you idiot. And now he knows you fancy him. Oh crappity crap.

"I'd like to get out of this suit," he added, loosening the knot of his red silk tie. "We had a meeting in Geneva fresh from the plane but between you and me, ties are like small talk."

"Oh?" Tash's mind felt curiously blank of words of more than one syllable.

Between you and me. You and me.

The words, combined with the idea of him getting out of his suit, stirred delicious possibilities in her mind. Perhaps this was Nate's superpower - turning the minds of all females to goo?

"They are both necessary evils." Nate grinned again, a flicker of knowing in his eyes told her he knew exactly what effect he had on her. It made something flip low down in Tash's stomach.

"Right, well...If you follow me I'll show you your bedroom," Tash blurted and turned, leaving the room. She assumed he was following her down the corridor, someone certainly was. But she didn't dare look back to check in case he was too close behind her. In case the bizarre connection he had straight to certain parts of her body made her do something really crazy like step even closer so she could inhale his masculine scent or nuzzle his neck.

Grip Tash. As in get one.

She walked down to the largest guest suite. She knew this room had been earmarked for him. There'd been enough fuss about what papers and magazines to leave for him on the small table in the corner - *Le Monde,* the *Financial Times, Vanity Fair* and *GQ.* Whether to leave an espresso machine in the room - no, too B&B. And whether orange blossom oil in the diffuser was too girly - at this point Scott had told Holly to stop fussing; Nathaniel Campbell was here to assess the business opportunities and write a book and being male meant he probably wouldn't even notice there *was* an oil diffuser in the room, never mind care what scent was in it.

Tash held the door open for Nate, surreptitiously inhaling his masculine, citrusy scent as he passed. Sod the orange blossom, she'd be happy to just to smell him all day. She walked into the room with him, embarrassed at her thoughts.

"Your, er bed." Tash gestured towards the king size sleigh bed, feeling vaguely stupid. "Sorry, I never know how to show people their rooms without sounding like a twat. Holly usually does this bit. As far as I'm concerned a bed is a bed and if you can't work out the difference between the ensuite and a wardrobe or work the switch for the blinds well...you don't deserve to have it pointed out to you. Not *you* obviously, I wouldn't imagine for a minute that... I think I'll just shut up now."

Argh. What is happening to me? This is not like me.

"I quite agree." Nate laughed and her chest relaxed in relief. "I hate it when hotel staff insist on showing me how my room works. I always want to tell them to sod off and leave me in peace."

Tash wanted to say 'me too' but then she'd never actually stayed in a hotel. The odd cheap guesthouse and B&B but nothing grander than that.

See? We have nothing in common. Nothing.

"So, everything's okay?" She hovered, pulling her arms across her chest again, not wanting to adopt a defensive posture but not knowing what else to do with her arms.

Does he want me to sod off?

"Everything seems great," Nate said, feeling the mattress with one hand while staring straight at Tash. "Nice and firm, just how I like it. How about you?"

"Um..." Tash's body had heated up so much she half wondered if she had a temperature. She wasn't a novice when it came to sexual tension or flirting. In fact she considered it her specialist subject but this... Never had she felt so jumpy, so physically jolted by an attraction and it was freaking her out.

This really won't do.

She was used to being the one in control, not the one being played. Sex meant very little to her. It had always been a currency, a source of power, a way to get physical affection and sometimes even to get a roof over her head.

"I only get a bunk bed to sleep in so I'm probably not the right person to ask." She stood rooted to the spot, her gaze fixed on the mattress where Nate had patted it.

"Is that right?" Nate asked, eyebrows raised.

About the bunk bed or not being the right person? Damn, does he think I've just told him I'm not interested?

Nate pulled his red tie off and flung it onto the bed, maintaining eye contact as the silence stretched taut between them. The corners of his mouth twitched; he was playing her all right.

All Tash could think about was Nate using that tie to bind her wrists while he bent her over the bed and did very bad things to her.

She blinked hard, trying not to gape at Nate as he discarded his jacket. Beneath his shirt she could see he was as fit as she'd first thought. Gym body, rugby playing fit. Hard taut muscles fit.

Oh God.

She inhaled deeply, trying to locate her sanity. Wishing she had the small talk gene after all.

It's just sexual desire. Someone's turned the dial up on the intensity, that's all.

She'd always assumed people were exaggerating when they used words like 'irresistible' or talked about love at first sight. It wasn't love, how could it be if you didn't even know the person? It was a primeval response to mate, a need just like hunger or thirst.

It just went to show it meant nothing if she was experiencing these...feelings for a man like Nathaniel Campbell who had nothing in common with her, nothing to do with her world.

Focus. I need to do what Holly said, do it well and not let my hormones distract me. That's all.

"So, you want me to show you Verbier?" She asked brightly.

He looked at her, amused, appraising her as his gaze travelled the length of her body. She felt it on her legs, her neck, her lips, her breasts... Her skin prickled as though it were a physical touch and he were stripping her. There could be no mistake, no other

21

interpretation, no innocent meaning in that look.

It was both an announcement and an invitation.

Boy, he really doesn't hang about does he?

Maybe she ought to be annoyed, to protest, but what would be the point? It wasn't like directness offended her; it was her preferred method of communication after all.

He knows I fancy him and he's playing me. But weirdly, I don't mind. I don't mind one little bit.

"I want you to show me everything," he replied quietly in a low tone that set Tash's pulse racing.

Chapter 3

"Oh?" The word barely made it out of her mouth, all the air in her lungs had mysteriously vanished. She stared at the dark chest hair visible at the exposed neck of his formal white shirt, her cheeks burning.

"But there's one thing I need to be upfront about Tash." Nate's tone changed from flirtatious to serious.

"What's that?" She continued to clutch her arms across her body, as though that might protect her from the force of nature that was Nate Campbell.

"My work is everything to me," he said. "Fun always has to come second. And I don't do complicated, I haven't time for complicated."

Huh?

A stirring of indignation at his presumption rose above the haze of sexual desire.

"Aren't you making a bit of an assumption here?" She narrowed her eyes into a fierce expression that usually cowed lesser mortals. "We've just met and I thought we were talking about me showing you around Verbier?"

He laughed then, eyes sparking with good humour. "And I thought you didn't do all that small talk bullshit? I like you and you like me. We both know it so what's the point in pretending otherwise? Scientists have proven we know if we're attracted to someone within ninety seconds to four minutes of meeting them. Fact. Why waste time sending oblique signals? We can have fun if you like, or not. It's up to you."

He shrugged as though he could take her or leave her, it was all the same to him and Tash's hands itched to slap him. And then rip his clothes off.

"Actually, you know, you were right." Tash smiled as sweetly as she could manage and backed towards to the door.

"Oh?" Nate unbuttoned his shirt, his smile sexy and confident

Tash swallowed hard at the bare chest he revealed, at the hair snaking down from taut, toned muscles into the waistband of his tailored suit trousers. Was he actually planning to strip in front of her? Ask her to do it here and now while the others were just in the next room? It was tempting to wait and see just how much he was going to strip off.

Maybe this was a test or some kind of stupid joke? Perhaps he was hoping to shock her.

As if.

Shock tactics were Tash's usual move. She couldn't help but admire him for stealing her moves.

And hate him.

God, I'm in trouble.

"I think small talk *is* sometimes necessary. Not bothering with it can be...rude." Tash said, wrenching her eyes away from Nate's naked torso.

He heaved a pretend sigh and sank down onto the bed. "Okay, like I said, I can do small talk when necessary. Later maybe. In the meantime could you see if you can get my luggage sent to my room? My PA knows which bags I need. Thanks."

Dismissed.

How had he turned her excellent put-down into a command for her to obey him in under a minute?

It was almost impressive.

Tash turned and did something totally alien to her nature - she fled, not bothering to stay to try and have the last word. Nate's low chuckle tickled her spine and turned her legs to jelly.

Shit, that man is dangerous. I shouldn't even be thinking about playing his games. It's crazy. I need to remember it's just hormones. If I can't control them then I'm as shallow as Rebecca.

Tash groaned aloud and dashed into the hallway cloakroom, running cold water onto her hands to chill them and then pressing her palms against her hot cheeks. It was tempting to respond to Nate's advances, however dangerous. And despite what she'd said, she liked that he hadn't wasted any time. After all the 'he likes me, he likes me not' type of crap men usually put you through, his take was refreshing.

But it was still too risky. Scott and Holly had given her a permanent base. She didn't quite dare call Chalet Repos a home but it was all she had. She couldn't compromise it for a meaningless fling with a man who stripped you naked with his eyes and then mentally got to the part where he casually dumped you, all in the space of a few minutes.

Maybe having sex with Nate could be viewed as helpful by Scott and Holly because I'll be keeping him happy?

But, much as Tash wasn't precious about sex, it was just a mutually enjoyable pastime after all, that idea still felt a little... demeaning. Like maybe he'd presumed she was provided for his entertainment.

You feel cheap. Maybe you look cheap too.

Tash felt jumpy as she went to relay Nate's instructions about his luggage to Holly. She wasn't entirely sure which of the group was Nate's PA even, it might be one of the men after all, not necessarily the woman. Once she'd passed the message on, she made her way to the kitchen.

"Wow, hot or what?" Amelia leant against the kitchen counter, eyes gleaming.

"Who?" Tash asked casually.

"Nathaniel Campbell of course." Amelia stared at her, incredulous.

Great, so the Nate Effect had infected all the females at Chalet Repos. The impulse to resist the mass hysteria competed with a hot rush of jealousy. Nate already felt like hers.

Except of course he wasn't, and never would be, even if she got into his bed.

"You've got a fiancé. He's called Matt, remember?" Tash replied sharply. How many times would she have to remind Amelia of that fact over the next month?

Amelia rolled her eyes.

"He's even sexier in real life than he is on TV." Rebecca leant back against the kitchen counter next to Amelia, sighing, her eyes dreamy.

"Is anyone going to help me with the baking for later? The world hasn't ground to a halt and I assume we still need cakes for tea." Tash's jaw clenched. She'd be grinding her teeth at night again if she wasn't careful. The constant low level irritation seemed ever present nowadays, anger simmering dangerously close to the edge. Holding herself back from the tipping point was a constant effort and she was getting tired of it.

Lucy appeared to be relatively unaffected at least. She had already pulled the flour and sugar containers out from the cupboards.

"What did you think of him then Lucy?" Tash asked, getting out the mixing bowl, needing a dose of Lucy's no-nonsense take on life to counter the collective star-struck swooning going on.

"He's very handsome and he's certainly got the charm." Lucy shrugged. "But he's hardly partner material, is he? All men like that are obsessed with one thing."

"Sex, you mean?" Tash asked.

"No," Lucy replied. "Their work. They'll never put you first, if they even remember you exist once they've shagged you that is."

"Sounds like you're talking from experience?" Tash raised an eyebrow, Lucy generally kept her emotions to herself and she'd

26

not hooked up with anyone all season. It seemed crazy to Tash to wait forever for someone special to come along who might never turn up. All men seemed pretty much the same anyway when you got down to it.

At least they had done until today.

"Yeah." Lucy smiled sheepishly. "Been there, done that and got the sodding T-shirt. Workaholics can only really focus on one thing at a time and that kind of drive makes them successful but it also makes them lousy partners."

It confirmed what Tash thought deep down. Hell, Nate had even said as much. He'd made it clear up front. So why did she feel so disappointed?

She caught Rebecca's curious gaze. Had Rebecca guessed that the Nate Effect had claimed another victim?

Great.

Now Tash was going to have to pretend she didn't like Nate to save face. If she could be bothered that was. She sighed. What would Rebecca and Amelia think if they knew what had just happened in Nate's room? What *had* just happened anyway? It could've been a game or harmless flirting.

Tash pursed her lips.

"Shall we make your yummy lemon drizzle cake Tash?" Lucy asked. "That's always a great hit."

Tash nodded. "And shortbread as well I think, it's nice and quick and we can head for the ski lifts before the queues get too bad."

"You'll have to make the most of any free time today," Rebecca said excitedly. "You and I are taking the group to the Snowpark tomorrow. Scott says we need to cram everything in around their schedule. We're also going with them to the W tomorrow evening for drinks."

Tash grimaced, even though normally the idea of an evening of free drinks at the W would have her punching the air. Having to spend so much time in Nate's company was going to make it seriously difficult to resist him. A new worry had been nagging at her. Had he been so upfront with her because he'd heard she had a 'reputation'? She'd read in a magazine that successful men had higher testosterone levels and were highly sexed. Perhaps Nate needed regular sex and thought she'd be an easy source.

So what if she'd slept around a bit? She was evolved enough to have discarded any sexual hang ups long ago. If less enlightened people chose to call her names because of it she really didn't give a toss.

Really.

Tash ignored the uncomfortable twist in her stomach and lifted the scales down from the shelf. She was good at ignoring things. It was something else she'd had lots of practice at.

"Why don't you come and sit next to me?" Holly asked, sitting by the fire later that evening. "Nate has been asking about Verbier's attractions."

"I was just going to help with the coffee." Tash hovered in the doorway.

"I'm sure it doesn't need three of you." Holly raised her eyebrows a fraction.

Too polite to remind everyone it's not actually my turn to make coffee tonight.

Tash walked towards the sofa slowly, scanning to see where to sit that wasn't too close to Nate. She slid in on the other side of Holly rather than next to Nate on the sofa opposite.

"Where is everyone?" She asked.

"Greg and Rob have gone out for a drink," Scott replied.

"And Madeleine's having an early night," said Nate. "So how long have you been in Verbier, Natasha?"

Tash hesitated, certain he was mocking her by using her full name. Yet she felt very aware of Scott and Holly next to her, willing her not to react. They couldn't understand just how much she hated the name Natasha. Or why.

Play nice. Show them you can be professional.

"About three and half years now." She crossed her arms over her chest, aware it made her look defensive but unable to stop.

"So she knows the place pretty well," Scott added.

Tash felt like she was being sold. Why? Did Nate need convincing she was up to showing him around?

Maybe he is having second thoughts about me.

Why did that thought make her feel so bad? Hadn't she decided sleeping with him would be trouble?

"She's also au fait with the experience days we've been introducing this season and has accompanied clients on the trips." Holly added.

"Yes, they sound great, although I am going to have to get my head down to work a lot this month."

"That's no problem," Scott replied. "We can be flexible around your schedule as we discussed and we can take you up to look at those plots of land whenever you like."

Nate nodded but turned to look back at Tash. "So, what did you do before you came to Verbier, Natasha?"

Her jaw tensed. "I was travelling in Europe, doing seasonal work here and there. I came here because I fancied skiing and it was the only way I could ever be able to afford it."

"But you stayed?" He asked. "Why?"

"Because I love the skiing, the scenery, the fresh air. And the après ski isn't too bad either." She quirked a smile. Maybe this was more about finding out about the resort than grilling her.

"But where did you grow up?" he asked.

Or maybe not...

"England."

"Yes," Nate persisted. "I can tell, but whereabouts?"

Tash's skin pickled. "All over, I doubt very much I've lived anywhere you might be familiar with."

"Have any of your team been to the Swiss Alps before Nate?" Holly interrupted politely.

She knows I don't talk about my past.

Thankfully Rebecca and Lucy brought the coffee in at that point. Tash didn't even care when Rebecca sat down next to Nate.

Let them talk about all the lovely places and people they have in common.

Tash tuned out, her jaw clenching tightly.

Why do I care what he thinks about me? Why?

She must've turned soft, staying in one place, making friends, trusting people... Why had she ever truly believed she could pull this off – this normal kind of life?

Hadn't she learnt by now that just when you got comfortable, something or someone came to yank the rug out from beneath your feet? Unless you kept moving and maintained your distance from people. Then no one got the opportunity to do that to you.

That's the theory anyway.

Although every fibre of her being screamed to let Nate do whatever he wanted to her, a niggling fear had triggered her fight or flight instinct. It would be impossible to keep Nate at a distance.

Too many questions, plus the kind of arrogance that always expects answers equals trouble.

"Okay Tash?" Holly whispered, linking an arm through the crook of Tash's elbow and leaning towards her.

"Yes, of course." Tash forced smile to her face, hating the anxiety in Holly's expression.

I wish she didn't worry about me so much.

But was that true, really? After all it wasn't that great when no one worried about you. A twinge of guilt reminded her why it really bothered her. She didn't want to cause Holly any extra stress, especially not now she was pregnant.

"Are you sure?" Holly whispered.

"I'm a big girl now Holly." Tash smiled.

Holly squeezed Tash's arm and released it, turning to reply to something Scott had said.

Tash caught Nate's eye. He stared at her hard, as though getting her measure. Just as she was about to look away he winked and grinned. The cheeky smile transformed his face, making it more playful, relaxed, flirtatious...

Tash closed her eyes briefly.

I have to get out of here.

"Excuse me, I just have to..." She murmured to whoever might be listening. Thankfully a loud discussion about Verbier's best bars was now in progress.

I could slip out to Bar des Amis.

After all, she'd be at the W tomorrow night and Holly hadn't actually asked her to stay in tonight. Tash had just decided it might be good to stay sober given she had to play tour guide tomorrow. But now a drink or two seemed like exactly what she needed. Maybe even some company.

No, scratch that. You know there's only one man you want to go to bed with...

She grabbed her jacket and was slipping into her boots when she felt a hand pressing against the small of her back.

"Going out?" Nate's voice behind her made her jump.

She swung around. A mistake, as now she was face to face with him. Too close.

"I'm meeting a friend," she said. It wasn't exactly a lie; she would be bound to see Sophie, Sophie just wasn't expecting her.

"Shame," he raised an eyebrow. "So you didn't like my attempts at small talk?"

"No, I..." Tash stared down, nervously fingering the fabric of her jacket.

He laughed. "Relax."

She looked up then, directly into his eyes. "Are you kidding?"

He stroked the side of her face with surprisingly gentleness. Then he lowered his mouth, his lips lightly brushing hers.

Unable to resist she parted her lips and he increased the pressure.

She reached up and kissed him back, her tongue meeting his.

Her body fizzed, all the reasons she didn't want to do this became hard to remember now. His hands on her back felt strong

31

and masterful. It was easy to imagine what else they might be capable of. Then she heard the murmur of voices from further down the hallway.

What am I doing?

She pulled back, suppressing the disappointment that he let her go without protest.

"I need to get going." She shrugged her jacket on, not meeting his eye.

"I'm looking forward to tomorrow," Nate replied, his tone calm. "It should be fun. The Snowpark I mean."

Tash slipped out of the door, heart pounding and nerves jangling.

She was going to need that drink.

Nate put his snowboard in the rack and couldn't help grinning at the stunned expression on Tash's face. He'd known exactly what she had thought of him when they met. He was good at summing people up. His first impression was invariably correct. He knew that right now the discovery he was a better snowboarder than her was absolutely killing her.

"So where did you learn to do that then?" Tash asked, lips tight, slinging her own snowboard into the rack as she gestured back towards the Snowpark jumps. "I thought work was...your only focus."

He shrugged. "Why Natasha, your small talk skills are really coming on."

Nate's grin widened at the barely disguised outrage flashing in Tash's cat-like eyes. Watching her efforts to control herself and plaster a polite smile on her face was really very funny.

She was so easy to wind up and she was definitely bringing out the devil in him, the part of him that liked to play. He was attracted to her, but there was something more than basic sexual attraction going on here. She had a barely disguised wildness and deeply ingrained irreverence he found extremely refreshing.

He liked her. He'd been struck by the spark of intelligence and humour in her eyes. He'd met girls like her through his charity projects. Girls who'd been overlooked or thrown a curve ball by life - they wore a brittle hardness like body armour but that toughness nearly always disguised a massive insecurity. Tash was tough, intriguing, infuriating and pretty damn sexy.

The dash of vulnerability thrown into the mix made her irresistible.

He almost wished she wasn't. There was a tonne of work to do on the book if he was going to meet the publisher's deadline. It was important he got it right. He also had to keep a close eye on the mentoring programming, as well as appraising the potential of the luxury chalet investment scheme.

There simply wasn't the time for a shagathon.

Because if he took Tash to bed there was no way he'd make do with a quickie.

Although, looking at her now, her eyes flashing and cheeks flushed from the winter sun... Well a quickie seemed like a very good idea. He felt like taking her right here on the snow behind the snowboard rack, or finding a deserted hut somewhere.

"My name is Tash," she ground out. The effort to be polite looked like it was killing her. "No one calls me Natasha."

He merely raised an eyebrow, mentally storing away the information that this was something that seriously bothered her. It piqued his interest. In his experience girls who changed their names and dyed their hair weird colours had seriously complicated stuff going on inside their heads.

Complicated was something he really didn't have time for. So, logically, he should take a step back, stop flirting.

I don't want to stop. I need this. You know what they say about all work and no play...

And oh boy, did he want to play with her.

"Okay Tash, in answer to your question I used to ski in the French Alps but I haven't had much opportunity to snowboard

33

lately. I've been too busy and the scarcity of mountains in London is a bit of a problem." He grinned. "So I'm a little bit rusty."

"Hmm." Tash narrowed her eyes but the corners of her perfect lips twitched and he wondered what it would be like to taste her, or to have those lips circling his cock.

He stifled a groan at the thought, his gaze raking Tash for a green light to see if she was up for it. Her pupils were certainly dark and dilated, there was no doubt she wanted him too. No amount of pink eye shadow and smoky eyeliner could disguise the sexual desire smouldering in her eyes.

And sex with her would be fantastic. He was sure of it.

Wasn't it a bit of a cliché though, sleeping with the chalet girl?

Oh who gives one? Since when did I care what people thought about my personal life?

"So...are you saying you never have time for...fun?" Tash arched an eyebrow. Her lips parted a little.

So, she was teasing him now was she?

"If there's a good enough incentive then I make time." He shrugged. In his peripheral vision he could see the others staring at them from the deck of the mountain cantine where they waited for Nate and Tash to join them. He knew Madeleine's expression would be one of disapproval, but then she didn't do fun, not that Nate could tell. She was good at her job which was what mattered and she knew better than to verbalise her disapproval.

Let them speculate. I really don't care.

"So, you need an excuse to do what you like then?" Tash asked, hunger flickering in her eyes.

It was a craving he knew exactly how to sate, a hunger that wouldn't be satisfied with a helping of cantine apple strudel.

"No," Nate said, making a snap decision. He wanted Tash. At this rate wanting her could easily become more of a distraction than sleeping with her ever could. Adrenalin trickled into his veins and his muscles tensed with anticipation. "I have to prioritise, but sometimes I do exactly what I like. I have...fun. How about you?"

34

Tash opened her mouth to answer but then the other chalet girl, the posh blonde one, strode across the snow to where they stood and Tash abruptly closed her mouth and looked away, staring at the mountaintops.

"Come and join us, we're ordering vin chaud, such a cliché but you need the full Verbier experience." The blonde girl grinned a little maniacally, nervous and probably unaware she was intruding on a private moment.

What was her name? Becky...Becca...

"Rebecca?" Nate took a guess at her name and when she didn't correct him he assumed he'd got it right. "We'll be right over, thanks."

Rebecca hesitated, biting her lip.

"Order a couple of glasses for us." He added more firmly, aware of the tension in the atmosphere but not sure where it was coming from, after all he'd barely exchanged two sentences with Rebecca since he'd arrived.

Rebecca walked away, frowning and Nate raised his eyebrows. "I think we're in trouble. Going AWOL will not be tolerated."

Tash grinned. "I've spent my whole life in trouble and believe me, it's not all that bad."

He laughed and walked with Tash over to the cantine decking.

Madeleine was tight lipped with disapproval when they arrived and sat down at the trestle table but then she and Tash were polar opposites in their lifestyle choices. Greg and Rob seemed oblivious to any tension; they were drinking vin chaud, enjoying the warm winter sun and why not? They'd all been working hard enough recently to deserve some downtime. Having the odd afternoon of relaxation wasn't going to kill him. He couldn't remember the last time he'd had a holiday. Anyway, didn't most people take two whole days off each weekend?

"So what's in the schedule for this evening?" he asked.

"After dinner we're going to show you Verbier at its most stylish, the aspirational scene we're trying to sell to all our prospective

35

clients," Rebecca said, with a slight arch of her eyebrow.

"In other words we're going to the W," Tash cut in.

"The cocktails are to die for." Rebecca added with an eager smile. She reminded him of a puppy.

Must be all that breeding.

In his world, over bred pedigree puppies were plentiful. Wildcats like Tash were much rarer.

And much more fun to tame.

"Yeah, you die of shock when you see the bill." Tash laughed. "Well normal people do anyway."

Normal people?

"Sounds like my kind of place." Greg smiled at Tash. "Looks like we're going to have a fun night."

Tash choked on a mouthful of vin chaud and caught Nate's eye.

A sharp jolt of connection passed between them and caught him off guard, sending a pulse of sexual electricity straight to his groin.

Cocktails, a hotel and some downtime with Tash. Now that sounds like a plan.

Tash sipped at her champagne cocktail while glancing around at the clientele. Most were dressed in outfits costing more than she made in six months, even more if you counted the handbags. It was après ski but not the kind she could afford or was accustomed to. There wasn't a ski bum or any of the instructors she knew in sight, instead there were chic groups of trustafarians and wealthy older couples dressed in head to toe cashmere. All quaffing champagne or expensive cocktails.

Rebecca had already bumped into three people she'd known at school.

Typical.

Chilled music filled the room and the seating areas covered with soft faux-fur throws were comfortable. Too comfortable. It would be easy to get used to this.

She stared at Nate. He'd merely nodded his approval at the

ultra trendy, luxury hotel rather than been bowled over by it. But of course *he* would be used to this.

We come from different worlds; I need to remember that.

And yet, couldn't she pretend, for just one evening, that they were here at the W on an equal footing? Just a man and a woman who'd met and felt an... attraction for each other.

I mustn't be naïve. I'm way down the food chain from Nate.

She couldn't help but feel flattered. Nate was easily the most striking man in the Living Room, the main bar of the W Verbier. Not necessarily the most handsome man but his aura of power added to his attraction. Wherever they'd been today heads turned in his direction and now the hotel guests and bar clientele stared as though wondering who he was, sure he must be someone they should know.

And he had chosen to sit next to Tash, so close their thighs were touching. He and Greg were discussing the stability of the Swiss franc and Tash had tuned out, aware only of the warmth of Nate's leg burning her through the fabric of her little black dress.

Not that it was her LBD. She hardly ever wore dresses so had borrowed it from Lucy. As Lucy was only five foot two and Tash was five foot six the hemline rode daringly high up her thigh. Holly had nodded her approval when she'd seen the outfit and told her to have fun.

Fun. There was that word again...

It wasn't as though Holly and Scott banned them from sleeping with the guests. Their view had always been that what consenting adults got up to was their own business. But this felt like new territory.

Tash was well and truly out of her comfort zone.

She took another sip of her cocktail, a divine concoction of fresh strawberries and champagne, savouring the taste. Then she caught Rebecca's baleful stare from the seat opposite her where she sat next to Madeleine. It was loaded with accusation. Tash knew what the look meant. *You said you weren't interested so what do you think you're doing making a play for him? He's mine...*

Except of course he wasn't Rebecca's. Tash doubted he'd ever be anybody's. He was, quite simply, his own man. She'd never got what that phrase meant until now. Self-contained and supremely confident, he inspired in you a desire to impress, to capture his short, 'suffer no fools,' attention span. Because, when you were the focus of his attention, it felt like basking in a sudden patch of sunlight with champagne cocktail fizzing through your veins, electrifying your nerve endings.

Tash guessed if you didn't rate with him in the first thirty seconds of conversation he'd move on. Politely of course, he was a gentleman after all. He'd be respectful but you'd have lost his attention, that full on blaze of charisma.

"Rebecca?" Nate turned towards Rebecca with a smile.

"Yes?" She leant forward in her seat, lips slightly parted, petulance forgotten. Maybe she was hoping to be asked her opinion on the Swiss franc?

"Would you do me a favour and take Madeleine, Robert and Greg for a look round the hotel?" Nate asked, easy charm in his smile. "I know Madeleine is very keen to see the spa."

Madeleine's pursed lips and minuscule nod didn't exactly exude keenness. She'd barely spoken to Tash and didn't seem to approve of her. But Madeleine couldn't sour the excitement now building in Tash.

"Of course." The instinctive response had escaped Rebecca's lips before she seemed to register this would leave Nate and Tash alone. Her smile slipped.

"I'd be very grateful," Nate added, upping the wattage of his own smile.

Rebecca's expression softened.

Nate was good.

And I'm going to be alone with him. He doesn't waste much time does he?

But then weren't entrepreneurs supposed to be risk takers?

They saw what they wanted and they went for it. Her stomach flipped at the thought and delicious anticipation bubbled inside her, fizzing like the exquisite champagne cocktail on her tongue.

Right now she'd do anything Nate wanted.

Anything.

Rebecca had no chance of resisting his will.

Tash didn't meet Rebecca's eye as Rebecca left with Madeleine, Robert and Greg. Guilt mingled with resentment inside her. No. Rebecca didn't get to have 'first dibs' on Nate because they weren't sixteen-year-olds. Rebecca wasn't entitled to Nate; she already had the large home in Surrey, the wealthy parents, the choice to work 'for fun' and even an effing pony.

Nate pressed his thigh harder against Tash's leg and she exhaled sharply.

"So." Nate turned to face her, his grin so confident that part of her wanted to walk out, just to show him he wasn't all that.

Except he *was* all that.

She'd googled him this afternoon and read how he built up his businesses from nothing and all about his charity work supporting young entrepreneurs. He'd set up a mentor scheme so young people with no connections, money or academic qualifications could turn their lives around. He probably rescued orphaned puppies in his spare time and helped old ladies across the road too.

Damn.

How could she resist him? She'd wanted to dismiss him as a stuffy suit, or as a greedy businessman but it turned out he reinvested a large percentage of his profits back into his charity work. And he'd never been part of the privileged trustafarian crowd she despised.

In fact he made her wonder what the hell she was doing with her life. He had six years on her, sure, but when he'd been her age he'd already made his first million.

What had she to show for her life so far?

"So?" She mimicked him, raising an eyebrow. Even if she didn't feel cool, she could act it. There was no need to show him how out of her depth she felt. 'If in doubt, just wing it' was a policy that'd served her well in the past.

"Do you want to do that small talk thing now then?" he asked, casually draping an arm over her shoulder and drawing her closer. His warm fingers brushed against the bare skin of her upper arm, making her tingle.

"Um, not really." Tash blinked, flattered he felt able to be so direct with her but distracted by the head spin that was being physically close to Nate.

Why am I making such a big deal out of this? It's only sex.

Usually she prided herself on being forward thinking and hang-up free when it came to sex. But there would be nothing 'only' about sex with Nate, she was sure of it. This felt like a really big deal. But a good big deal. She might only have him for one night but it would be worth it.

Would Holly definitely be okay with this?

She doesn't need to know.

Tash dismissed the vague sense of unease. Keeping Nate happy had to be a good thing surely?

She dismissed her concerns and turned her full attention back to Nate, to the amused twist at the corner of his lips and the wicked glint in his eyes that made her want to drop her knickers here and now.

"You don't want to tell me about your pet rabbit?" He asked, fingers lightly massaging her shoulder.

"No pets." She stared into his eyes, ever surprised by the sense of connection she found there. It made her want to bind herself to him, to become a part of him with a fierce intensity that shocked her.

"What about pesky older brothers tying your pigtails to chair backs?" Nate's hand snaked up beneath her hair to stroke the nape of Tash's neck.

"None of those either," she replied. "Brothers I mean, or sisters.

I'm a sibling free zone in fact."

It was sort of true.

I never should've had that third cocktail.

But without it she might not have found the courage to do this. This was not your average hook up.

"What were you like as a school girl?" Nate asked in a low tone. "Were you a good girl Tash?"

Tash grinned. "No, I was a very, very bad girl."

Nate raised an eyebrow, lips twitching into a sexy smile. "I can imagine."

"Then you have a filthy mind Mr Campbell," Tash whispered, leaning closer into him, her body on fire where it met his, every muscle coiled tight with anticipation. "And how about you? What were you like at school?"

She crossed her legs towards him so her hemline rose even higher, he could see the beginnings of the lacy band of her hold-ups if he looked carefully. With a surge of triumph she saw he *was* looking very carefully indeed.

This feels better than any cocktail, better than a hundred cocktails put together.

"Oh I was very, very bad too." Nate's fingers caressed her neck, tracing tiny circles on her skin, a promise of what he might do to other parts of her body. "I was always mucking about, playing the class joker. Hanging out with the very, very bad girls behind the bicycle sheds."

"Oh?" Tash's breath caught at the top of her chest. "So what exactly did you do with them, behind those bike sheds?"

"I liked to tease them. I was very good at it. Would you like me to give you a demonstration?" Nate's other hand found its way onto her knee without her noticing.

Tash felt like she couldn't breathe at all. "That...would be...fun."

It was finally out there, the unspoken assumptions forcing themselves out into the open.

So we do have something in common after all. We're both rebels.

Despite Nate's suit and respectable outward appearance there still lay the rebellious instincts she knew only too well.

"Shall we get a room?" he asked.

Chapter 4

Nate massaged a knot in Tash's shoulders and she thought she might melt into a pool of lust right there on the floor.

She desperately wanted those fingers on her breasts and down between her legs. Like right now. Just the thought of it almost made her come.

"What, here at the W?" Tash gasped as he continued to stroke her neck and casually left his other hand resting proprietorially on her knee.

"Yes, unless you want everyone at Chalet Repos to know what we're up to and..." he lowered his mouth to her ear and dropped his tone to a whisper, "If you want them to hear you scream. I believe the rooms are better soundproofed here and I do intend to make you scream when you come."

She shuddered involuntarily, chest heaving and nipples tightening into hard buds as she jerked beneath his fingers, so turned on she wouldn't have stopped him if he'd fucked her right here in the bar in front of everyone.

"You're a bad man Nathaniel Campbell," she said, her voice a little breathless.

"Is that a 'yes' then?" he asked.

She took a deep breath and nodded.

"I'll go and sort it out." Nate disengaged himself and walked towards reception.

Tash, stunned, let her gaze travel over the rest of the bar clientele. Some of the uber-groomed women stared at her with undisguised jealousy, looking scornfully at her home dyed hair and borrowed high street dress in a 'what's so special about you?' way.

For once Tash actually had something in common with them in that she hadn't the foggiest. What had Nate seen in her?

Probably just thinks you're a tart, an easy source of sex.

The cruel thought taunted her, denting her newly growing confidence.

I don't care.

And when Nate beckoned her over, smiling, there wasn't any room in her head for anything except the one thought.

He wants me. He wants me. He wants me.

How she made it across the room without tripping and providing the onlookers with a floorshow she didn't know. Yet it seemed as though she were transported on air, every muscle taut with desire and aching with anticipation.

After they'd been shown to their room, the hotel staff member drifted tactfully away, not once commenting on the absence of luggage or giving any indication that he considered their reservation unusual. The room was called a 'Spectacular Room' and it lived up to its claim to embody sleek mountain chic. The combination of pine, grey slate, red leather and cowhide chairs worked well. The lights were tiny glass globes hanging down from the ceiling like a modern art installation.

Tash was just worried she might break something. She didn't like to think how much the room cost.

"What did you tell them?"

"That I needed the room for an hour because I'd met a sexy high-class call girl." Nate quipped.

Tash stared at him, rooted to the floor.

Nate laughed. "Muppet. As if. I told them it was a last minute decision, we'd been so impressed by the hotel we wanted to spend longer here."

"And they believed you?"

"Who cares?" Nate shrugged. "It's no one else's damn business. Now are we going to waste time with silly conversation or..."

"I think we'll go with 'or,'" Tash replied dryly. "God forbid we waste the precious time of the great Nathaniel Campbell."

For a second Nate stared hard at her. She held her breath. Then he barked with laughter and sat on the edge of the bed. "Come over here and say that," he dared her.

Tash reached round her back to unzip her dress first. It was a move she'd made many times before but this time her fingers trembled a little.

I can't let him see I'm intimidated. I have to try to take the lead. I must stay in control.

She stepped out of the pile of black viscose pooling around her feet and walked forward, glad to see from Nate's expression that she had his attention. Sexy underwear never failed. She was about to unhook her bra when he raised a hand.

"Stop," he said quietly. "I want to do that."

A little put out he'd interrupted her routine she crossed the last bit of rug separating her from Nate, less sure of herself now.

He parted his legs to make space for her and tugged her hard towards him. His strong thighs gripped her legs and the hand pressing against the base of her spine held her firmly against him. Then Nate lowered his lips to her stomach and kissed her. Desire jerked a response, pulsing between her legs. She wanted to wriggle free, to regain control but he wouldn't let her.

Then he spun her around and planted slow, hungry kisses against her spine, his hands reaching up to cup her lace-covered breasts. She moaned, feeling like jelly in his hands. Jelly that was slowly dissolving.

He tweaked one of her nipples and a corresponding dart of pleasure shot between her legs.

"Are you wet for me, Tash?" He whispered against her skin.

"Shall we find out?"

She shuddered again as he trailed his hands up between her legs, tracing the lacy edge of her knickers, teasing her through the fabric. Tash could barely breathe; she wasn't sure she'd still be standing if it weren't for his thighs pressed against her, holding her up. With a quick tug he pulled her knickers down her legs and his fingers plunged inside her, teasing and stroking at the wetness he found there.

When he withdrew his hand she parted her legs, arching her bottom back towards him, aching to feel his touch again. She didn't seem able to remember any of her normal moves, it felt impossible to regain control. He didn't touch her but she felt his hot breath like a shiver against her spine.

After what felt like an eternity he deftly unhooked her bra and it fell to the ground.

"Turn around," Nate ordered, his voice less in control than before as he released the grip of his thighs.

She turned, naked except for her heels and hold-up stockings. He'd removed his expensive shirt to reveal the perfect torso she'd been thinking about ever since she'd shown him to his room at Chalet Repos.

Eager to regain control she reached out to stroke his chest, oh so accidentally nudging her leg up against the huge erection now evident in his designer jeans.

He groaned as she sank to her knees, her fingers fumbling with his button fly. He helped her and soon he was naked too.

Only then did he kiss her, pulling her down so they lay in a tangle of limbs, her nipples pressing into his bare chest. Her fingers clutched at his back, pulling him against her as they kissed, tongue on tongue.

After a minute he pulled back, breathing hard. "Lie still."

The tone of his voice brooked no argument so Tash obeyed and lay, naked and panting on the now tangled white cotton sheets.

"Spread your legs," he commanded in a low voice.

She parted them for him but he grasped her ankles and yanked them further apart, stretching her wide open in front of him.

Her sex throbbed, desperate for his fingers, his mouth, his cock... "Please..." she whispered.

He stared, exhaling hard before climbing on the bed between her outstretched bare legs. He placed one hand on each of her thighs and then slowly lowered his head between her legs. The anticipation felt almost unbearable in its intensity.

She groaned when he lowered his mouth to her. As soon as his tongue licked her clit she jerked hard against his mouth, her hands weaving into his hair. As he kissed and teased her she felt like she was falling. She was so turned on, so tightly wound with anticipation that the waves of orgasm came almost immediately. She moved beneath his lips as he teased her relentlessly, drawing her orgasm out, pushing her further when she thought she couldn't take anymore, sending her spiralling out of control.

Once she could breathe again she rolled over, the soles of her feet still tingling. She wanted to repay him. Her breasts grazed his chest as she crawled on all fours, all the way down to his erection. She took him in her mouth and looked up at him. His eyes darkened and he let out a deep moan as he stiffened even more between her lips. She used her tongue to tease the tip of his erection, unusually she was almost as turned on as he was by the movement. She began to hum and was gratified when he groaned and swore.

Tash was good at this, she'd had a lot of practice but, and not that she'd ever admit it, she'd never really enjoyed giving oral. It was just something you had to do, a secret weapon to get men to like you, to be grateful. Sex had been a means to an end, a source of affection, a comfort or sometimes the only way to ensure a roof over her head.

A fair exchange. She was honest about it and didn't bother dressing it up in the way other people did. They were kidding themselves. Sex was always about an exchange of some kind.

It had never bothered her exactly but this...this felt different. Erotic, yes but also powerful and deep. Even, dare she think it, spiritual.

With Nate's rock-hard erection in her mouth she felt more turned on than she ever had in her life. She was wet between her legs again, slick with desire to have him deep, deep inside her. She wanted to withdraw now and straddle him. He was clearly close to coming though, so she made the unselfish choice; she would let him orgasm and then wait for him to recover.

One practiced flick of her tongue had him stiffening. She pulled back and rubbed his erection over her breasts, watching as he came hard on her flesh.

"Oh God...Tash," he groaned, half growled her name.

She crawled up his chest to lie on top of him, skin against skin. He was tall enough that her head fitted perfectly under his chin. She turned her head sideways, his heartbeat pulsed quickly under her ear. The sound, combined with the warm solid body beneath her felt comforting and she exhaled.

"That was just for starters," she whispered, tilting her face to look up at him.

"I'm looking forward to the main course. Is there a set menu?" He asked, wrapping his arms around her. "Or can we choose à la carte? What turns you on Tash?"

Tash considered. It wasn't something she spent much time thinking about. Usually she did her thing with the guy she'd gone home with and they were grateful, end of. She moved on before anyone could get more attached. Except that felt a little...shabby now. Utterly unsatisfying. The 'scratching an itch' analogy was now stretched so taut it was at snapping point.

How had she not known desire could be like this? So powerful it could consume you and make the rest of the world fade away to an irrelevance.

"I don't know." she muttered.

You do Nate. You turn me on.

She'd die before she admitted him taking control had been beyond sexy. But it had. Why else would she have come practically the second his tongue slipped between her legs?

She shifted her weight, wondering he had condoms with him, when he sat up and grabbed her wrist, staring and frowning.

"What's this?" Nate's voice was hard. He seemed angry.

Tash froze as she registered what he was staring at. Ice trickled down her spine, quashing the desire, dampening it. She stared down at his chest.

"Just a few scars," she mumbled, trying to yank her arm free.

"No it's not." He twisted her arm round into the light. "More than a few. You're a cutter. Or at least you used to be."

Tash stared at him, horrified, ashamed... Frozen in place she couldn't move, couldn't speak.

But no one ever notices. No one.

She'd worn long sleeves throughout her teens, even covering up in summer. But when the scars had faded and none of her hook ups seemed to notice when she was naked she'd stopped bothering. No one ever commented and she'd been sure nobody would notice unless they were really looking.

She inhaled sharply and tried to pull away but he wouldn't let her. She felt achingly naked, her emotions just as horribly exposed as her body, both stripped naked in front of him.

She blinked hard.

I will not cry.

"So, I used to self-harm when I was younger. So what?" She spoke between tightly clenched teeth, not meeting his eyes but instead staring down at his chest. "I don't do it anymore. End of."

What was the point of denying it? He'd noticed the scars.

He noticed.

She shrugged but hot tears still burned in her eyes, threatening to fall.

Don't you dare cry.

"Tell me why," he said, holding her firmly, refusing to let her

49

run away from him as though he knew that was what she'd do given the chance.

"No," Tash replied stubbornly, biting the inside of her lip. "Why does it bother you? I thought your philosophy was about leaving the past behind you and moving on? You're even writing a bloody book about it."

"Oh, so you've googled me have you?" Nate raised an eyebrow. "That means you know all about me, every bit of gossip and trivia, not to mention the working class background the media so love to harp on about. It also makes things a bit one-sided, doesn't it? Why don't you give me the google version of... Natasha, before she became Tash. What would that say?"

Tash sighed and stopped struggling. What was the point? Resisting Nate in any way felt futile. Plus she had a feeling a man like Nate could find out pretty much anything he wanted to. She needed to give him just enough so he didn't feel the need to go digging. She stared into his eyes, encouraged by the understanding she found there. There was no judgement, none that she could see anyway.

"It would say...Natasha was born to two parents, one of whom didn't want her and the other couldn't cope. So she was shunted off into a series of foster homes, fourteen in total." Tash kept her tone bland, trying to summon as much detachment from the words as she could, as though they weren't about her at all but about another girl. In a way it really felt like they were. That girl didn't exist anymore and she felt nothing for her. "Natasha wasn't cute enough or pretty enough or most importantly young enough to get picked for adoption so she learnt early on the only person she could rely on was herself."

Her jaw muscles were so tight they ached. She stared at Nate pleadingly. There was more. They both knew there was more to the story but right now Tash couldn't talk about it. Not even if she'd wanted to. The emotions were so powerful they rose up like a clenched fist, constricting her throat and choking her.

She saw herself through Nate's eyes then. Saw his appraisal of her 'notice me' pink-striped hair, her exaggerated 'look at me' eye make-up...and she wanted to crawl under a rock and never come out again.

He'd stripped her bare and, not content with that, he'd ripped her apart.

"Well, you've had your sob story, can I go now?" She glowered at him, her anger turning to numb detachment.

I won't talk about the cutting. I can't. No good can come of dredging up the past.

How could anyone who hadn't actually been through it understand? Would Nate understand a pain and anger so terrible they could only be appeased by physical pain and blood? Would he understand how you had to turn the anger inwards after it became obvious turning it against the world got you sod all except a reputation as a problem child?

And it helped. You felt better afterwards. Tash remembered that now as her teeth clenched so tightly she could hear her pulse beating hard in her ear. Buried memories fought hard to resurface, assaulting her senses. She could even smell the metallic tang of blood.

She squeezed her eyes tight shut, blinking away the memories, her free hand clutching a handful of cotton sheet.

Nate kept hold of her other wrist and leaned further towards her, still refusing to let her go.

What inane platitude would he come up with? Some people assumed self-harm was just a plea for attention. Yeah, so that would be why she'd managed so successfully to hide what she was doing from her foster parents, teachers, social workers and the odd psychiatrist or two then.

It was the only way I knew how to cope.

Instead Nate did the only right thing. He kissed her, deep and soft, stirring her deeply, making her want to bury her head into his chest and howl.

His tongue probed gently into her mouth and she found her jaw automatically unclenching as hot tears scalded her eyes. Somehow his kiss transcended the fierce pain and disarmed her. The horror of the memories receded a little, life affirming desire surging through her again as the hand not holding her wrist gently stroked her bare back.

Then he raised her wrist to his mouth and tenderly kissed the scars, trailing the kisses up her arm, over every tiny faded white line. That undid her. Tears finally burst the banks of her eyelids, flooding her cheeks. She ignored them, scarcely able to breath, totally unable to think.

When he pulled his lips away and looked up at her Tash steeled herself for a platitude again.

"You never did tell me what turns you on but I think I can guess."

"Oh?" Tash half laughed, half sobbed, relief surging through her that he wasn't going to torture her any more tonight.

"Yes." Nate trailed a finger along her breastbone. "You pretend you like to be in control but I think it turns you on when I tell you what to do. Although I bet you'd die sooner than admit it."

So maybe he is going to torture me a little.

But in a nice way, maybe...

"Hmm, there may be the teensiest bit of truth in that," Tash said, sniffing. A night of cutting her nose off to spite her face or a night of being turned on by Nate?

No contest.

"Shall we find out?" Nate grinned crookedly, his finger lightly tracing the outline of her breast, fleetingly grazing her budding nipple.

"Try your worst." Tash tried to inject cool into her tone but the words came out squeakily. "Or should that be your best?"

"I am rather good at telling people what to do." Nate raised his eyebrows.

"Yeah, I'm sure you get a lot of practice." Tash rolled her eyes at his smug tone but was forced to admit he was probably telling the truth. "So, what turns you on then?"

"Giving you pleasure is what turns me on." Nate maintained eye contact for a few seconds. "There's nothing sexier than watching a woman come."

Tash thought she might actually melt there and then on the expensive Egyptian cotton sheets. Nate rolled her over before slipping from the bed and walking over to the window. He came back with the expensive looking rope tiebacks.

"I'm also good at improvising," he added.

Tash's stomach performed its now familiar acrobatic routine. It was just as well she hadn't been able to eat much earlier.

She'd been tied up before and hadn't thought it was really her thing. With Nate though, the thrill of what he might do to her sent a sharp shiver of pure lust through her body. He bound her wrists to the headboard, the knots firm but not painful.

If he's trying to distract me it's working.

Then he disappeared to the bathroom, coming back with a small bottle of massage oil and a small white hand towel.

"They really do think of everything, don't they?" Tash murmured, shifting position on the bed, every nerve in her body electrified.

"Not quite, I couldn't find a blindfold so you're going to have to be a good girl and leave this towel over your eyes." He placed the towel on her face, it smelt clean, of washing detergent, and the cotton felt soft against her skin.

Tash hadn't appreciated how much not seeing would heighten the sensation of Nate's touch but when it eventually came her body practically convulsed beneath his firm fingers. He slowly peeled her stockings down her legs and then massaged oil into her calves and thighs, his hands sliding expertly over every inch of her skin.

His touch affirmed her, pushing back the tide of hurt. When he massaged up between her legs she gasped but he passed round and up onto her hipbone without touching her where she really wanted him to.

He knows how to tease.

Then he massaged her arms, her breastbone and eventually her breasts, rubbing his palms over her now erect nipples.

She wriggled, moaning as anticipation fizzed through her body but still he didn't relieve the pent up pressure throbbing between her legs.

Then suddenly his touch was gone.

"Hey, come back," she grumbled.

"I'll be back in a minute," Nate promised.

In alarm Tash tipped her head back in an attempt to dislodge the towel from her eyes. Peeking out from the bottom of the towel she could just make out Nate wearing a white hotel robe, walking towards the door.

"You're leaving me here?" Tash asked with disbelief, nibbling at her lower lip as scenarios flashed through her head. It wouldn't be the first time she'd got herself into a dodgy situation but she'd learnt to trust her instincts and she really hadn't felt that vibe from Nate.

Is he going to leave me here to be found by hotel staff? How well do I know him, really?

Yet, even though the answer to the last question should have been 'not at all' it felt like she did know him, could trust him. He might be a lot of things but she didn't think he was cruel. But trusting someone she barely knew? It went against all her usual defences.

I'm an idiot, I should know better than to be taken in by raging hormones and a bit of sexual chemistry. Okay, a whole lot of sexual chemistry.

As Nate's clothes were still in the room it seemed unlikely he'd legged it but the anxiety didn't leave her until a soft click indicated Nate had entered the room. A familiar clink of ice against metal made her wonder if he'd got champagne. Or...

"What exactly are you planning to do with that ice?" she asked, her tone suspicious. Yet secretly she was really, really turned on by the effort he was going to.

"You'll see, or rather you'll feel. No peeking." Nate tugged the towel back down over her eyes.

Tash lay, waiting, every nerve tingling with anticipation. When Nate's warm lips enclosed her left nipple without warning she shuddered, then shrieked when his mouth was replaced with an ice cube. Her nipple, hard as a pebble, throbbed a protest before her right nipple received the same treatment.

"You sod, that's freezing," she complained, kicking out at him with her bare foot.

"Trust me." He laughed, grabbing her ankle and holding her leg out to the side while he fleetingly trailed the ice cube down to her stomach and towards the heavy ache throbbing between her thighs.

She gasped, her body simultaneously tensing at the cold, melting beneath the hot tongue teasing her nipple and the sensation of warm, firm flesh pressed hard up against her. She could feel his erection pressing against her thigh and it distracted her from the ice cube's path down across her abdomen.

Then Nate lay half on top of her, trailing kisses up her neck. His lips found her mouth beneath the edge of the towel, smothering her gasp when he thrust another ice cube up inside her, holding it there for a second while his tongue thrust into her mouth. In a split second he'd removed the ice cube and was using it to slowly circle her clit.

Tash groaned and shrieked up into Nate's kiss, squirming beneath his fingers and the weight of his body, hating and loving it all at the same time.

As the ice melted against her hot, slick flesh, water trickled down between her legs onto the sheets. Tash cried out and squirmed, every muscle contracting, arching towards Nate. She longed to have her hands free, to caress his erection until he couldn't hold back any longer and had to thrust inside her. She wanted to dig her nails into the firm flesh of his buttocks, moving her hips to make him pump faster and harder and...

Oh...my...God...

Nate had crawled back down her body and when the ice cube was replaced by his hot lips sucking at her clit Tash screamed, limbs jerking as she came, wave upon wave of delicious pleasure racking her body as he teased her relentlessly. But even before the orgasm had subsided she knew it wasn't enough, she wanted Nate inside her.

"Fuck me. Please. Now," Tash half babbled, half groaned, not caring that she was begging. "You are driving me insane."

"Sure," Nate laughed again but his breathing sounded laboured, as though holding back had been a struggle.

Good.

"Trust me, it'll be my pleasure," he added, grasping both her ankles and parting her legs wide on the bed, shifting his weight so he lay between her legs. The tip of his erection brushed against her, making her still sensitive clit quiver.

A familiar crackle of a foil packet reassured her, although it hadn't exactly been at the front of her mind. More evidence she must be slightly out of her mind at the moment.

I'm lying naked, bound to a bed at the W with Nate Campbell between my legs while Rebecca takes the others on a tour of the spa... fricking hell, would she say if she knew?

"Oh!" she gasped as he thrust inside her. She'd been expecting it but he still took her by surprise. Not being able to see made the heightened sensations even more delicious.

She arched her back and wrapped her legs around him, pulling him deeper into her, heels digging hard into his buttocks. He filled her up and she revelled in the delicious friction. She felt exhilarated, surging on natural endorphins, the best natural high she'd ever known.

Scrub that, it's the best high I've ever known, chemical or natural.

"How do you want it?" Nate's breath was hot against Tash's neck, his evening stubble lightly grazing her skin.

"Hard," she whispered hoarsely, anticipation coiling tightly inside her, her muscles contracting around his erection. She sighed with pleasure at Nate's sharp intake of breath.

He thrust hard into her, each stroke jolting the bed so Tash's wrists jerked against the curtain ties. Her back arched towards him, hips responding instinctively.

"Harder," she gasped, feeling the familiar warm tide of another orgasm building inside her.

She needed this release, needed him to blot out all the savage emotion he'd awoken in her. Needed to be suffused with pure, life-affirming pleasure.

He pushed both her knees up onto her chest and thrust again, the angle even deeper than before. It felt like he were piercing her, like the orgasm building might rip her body in two.

"I need to see you," Tash groaned. "Let me see you fucking me."

Nate pushed the towel away with an impatient hand and Tash stared into his dark eyes, blinking hard, glad he'd left the lights on so she could see every straining muscle, watch the beads of perspiration sliding between their bodies.

"I'm close," she whispered.

Wordlessly he raised himself up slightly on one arm while slipping his other hand in between their bodies. He caressed her clit tenderly, the lightness of his touch a direct contrast to the force of his previous thrusts. Tash contracted hard around him, her body shuddering as she climaxed. Nate withdrew his hand and thrust into her as waves of pleasure racked her body. He came quickly, crying out her name as he stiffened and jerked inside her. Then he collapsed on top of her, his chest still heaving. He was heavy but she liked the reassuring bulk of his body covering hers.

"Christ, that was good." He sighed contentedly and withdrew, rolling down onto the bed next to her and disposing with the condom in a tissue with practiced ease.

Disposable. Like me?

"It was," Tash replied, suddenly feeling tired. "But...my wrists are hurting a bit, could you untie me?"

Post sex she felt vulnerable, the urge to escape pounding in her head now that her hormones had subsided.

"Of course," Nate untied her. "So, I was right then? You liked it?"

"Erm, yes, even the ice cubes but..."

"But what?" Nate raised an eyebrow.

"The bed's a bit of a mess," she blurted. "What on earth are the housekeeping staff going to think?"

"Who cares?" Nate shrugged, unbothered. "It'll be okay."

But then he'd never cleaned rooms before had he? The staff who worked in housekeeping were faceless, unimportant. Like chalet girls?

Like me?

It occurred to Tash he'd done this routine before, with other girls. Well, probably not the kissing the scars bit, but...who knew? What if that had just been part of breaking down her defences? Maybe he didn't want to know because he cared but because he was the kind of man who liked to have all the facts.

She resisted the thought that it'd be nice to have Nate for more than just one night. Usually sex got the first flush of a crush out of her system.

Not this time.

If anything it had intensified whatever this thing was she was feeling.

That's because this isn't just a crush.

She smothered the thought, it couldn't be more; more would leave her vulnerable, to hurt, rejection, abandonment...

But she wanted him more than ever. How could she go back to casual hook ups with sexy ski instructors? They seemed like boys compared to Nate. She'd been given a flukey upgrade.

You know what they say, it's hard to downgrade again, once you've experienced the best.

Tash rolled over and spoke quietly into Nate's shoulder. "Thanks for this evening Nate, it's been fun."

Had she hit the right tone of non-committal approval? She waited, but the only response from Nate was a loud snore.

So, he wasn't perfect after all, he snored.

Of course he snores, he's just a man. A man every bit as likely to let you down as any other, if not more so.

She had to remember she was just a temporary bit of fun. Chalet girl sex on tap. Good sex, but just sex. She ignored the surge of emotion in her chest that said there was something more than that here. He'd been the first lover to question her about her scars. There was that funny sense of connection too, whenever their eyes met.

It means nothing. You mean nothing to him. How could you ever imagine someone like you would?

Wordlessly, silently she slipped from the bed and scooped up her clothes.

Time to make an exit.

Chapter 5

Nate stared down at the cursor blinking in the open Word document on his laptop.

The blank Word document.

He had an outline, there'd been input from his editor at the publishers after all and he knew what he wanted to say. Just not how he was going to say it.

He seemed strangely unable to think, his mind full of images from the night before - Tash in the full throws of orgasm, Tash moaning into his mouth as he kissed and finger-fucked her at the same time, Tash blinking back tears as her brittle shell cracked open in his hands...

The scars had taken him by surprise. Maybe he wouldn't have recognised them for what they were if it weren't for the charities he was involved in.

It complicated things.

Nate sighed and flicked back to the email from his editor.

Come on, concentrate. This is exactly why you shouldn't have got involved.

He'd barely scanned two lines before he found himself staring at the wall in his guest room. He'd asked for a table and chair to be moved in here. Focusing was hard enough with Tash in his head, let alone right in front of him.

Why did she run out on me?

The obvious explanation was that she hadn't wanted to arrive back at the chalet at the same time as him, but a niggling voice said she'd actively run away from him.

A shag-and-run.

The fact he hadn't been able to get her alone since bothered him. The other two girls had been serving breakfast. Tash hadn't made an appearance. Madeleine had maintained an air of quiet disapproval, knowing better than to voice her opinions. He'd already made it perfectly clear to her that his private life was entirely his business.

Women were so skilled at letting you know what they thought without opening their mouths though and those pursed lips were getting on his nerves. Any more attitude from her and he was going to have to have a word.

A knock at his door jolted him from his thoughts.

"Come in," he snapped, irritated by yet another distraction from the task at hand.

"Everything okay Nate?" Madeleine entered the room, dressed in her formal trouser suit. He wondered if she even owned a pair of jeans.

"Fine," he replied curtly.

"I wondered if you needed me to...have a word with the chalet girl, Natasha?" She slipped into the room and closed the door behind her. "It could get...awkward if she develops unrealistic expectations. I could handle that for you, make it easier?"

Madeleine nervously tucked a short curl behind her ear.

"You thought what?" He growled, narrowing his eyes at her. "Madeleine, have I ever given you cause to think I need your help in this area?"

"Well, I have sometimes had to fend off calls from certain women," she retorted. "It often becomes my business."

Nate ground his teeth. "Well I don't need your help now, thank you."

61

His words had been spoken with such a strong undercurrent of sarcasm she'd have to be stupid not to notice. And whatever Madeleine was, she wasn't stupid.

"Okay," she replied tightly, cheeks flushed a rosy pink. "Well if you change your mind just let me know. Can I get you some coffee?"

"Yes," Nate replied, jaw tight. "Thank you."

When she'd left the room he closed his eyes and exhaled deeply. So what if Madeleine didn't approve? Madeleine was a snob, he knew that much about her. He loathed this emerging class structure, this new upper class formed from an unholy trinity of privilege created by birth, privilege bought by wealth and privilege bestowed by fame. It was everything he was fighting against. It was the whole point of the *In the Lion's Den* programme and his mentor scheme.

It seemed the more successful he became, the more he was surrounded by people who cared about the distinctions. It was a far cry from the type of crowd he'd grown up with.

Some people weren't lucky enough to be born into privilege and for whatever reason failed to rise to the top for lack of opportunity. But with a little help and someone to believe in them...

Tash needs me to believe in her. But she's clearly damaged. Can she really cope with a short fling? What if I end up damaging her even more? Perhaps sleeping with her was selfish.

The whispered thoughts troubled him. If he said he hadn't time to deal with anything complicated, wasn't he being hypocritical? What was the point of writing the bloody book to help all these hypothetical people if he wasn't prepared to help an actual person who needed him?

Because the one thing he was sure of was that Tash did need him.

Nate opened the Word document again and began to write.

"Didn't take Nate long to avail himself of the facilities on offer, did it?"

Tash paused in the kitchen doorway with a full rubbish sack

62

in her hand when she heard someone talking.

That's Madeleine's voice.

She hesitated when the comment was followed by laughter. Listening at doors wasn't really her thing. Usually if she heard anyone talking about her she'd walk straight up to confront them, verbal attack being the best form of defence. But this time, being direct wasn't going to get her what she wanted - information.

"He's hardly going to take her to a Downing Street reception as his plus one, is he? Can you imagine?"

A male voice replied. "Perhaps she's going to be one of his *projects.*"

Tash wasn't sure who the second voice belonged to, but then it hardly mattered whether it was Robert or Greg. The comment stung. A familiar hardness crept into her heart and her features stiffened.

"Well she's not exactly going to be his girlfriend," Madeleine said scornfully. "Can you imagine? Highly unsuitable."

Teeth clenched, she entered the main living area to find Madeleine, Robert and Greg lingering over coffee at the table, laptops and BlackBerries strewn across the table.

"Hi guys, have you got everything you need?" Tash asked them briskly in an over-bright tone, forcing a smile to her lips.

They nodded, but only Greg had the grace to look abashed. Madeleine looked at Tash like she ought to be putting herself into the rubbish sack too.

Bastards.

"Great, well I'll just get on with taking out the rubbish then," Tash responded, making sure to hold her head high. She avoided the temptation to rearrange her fingers into a V sign on the rubbish sack. It was difficult to control her instincts but Holly and Scott came first.

They're right you know...

The whispered thought wouldn't go away.

They're right. They're right. They're right...

Tash gulped a deep breath of fresh mountain air at the back door. She didn't bother with a coat as the winter sun felt warm against her skin and there wasn't a cloud in the sky. She walked towards the area's communal rubbish collection point; what looked like a normal sized bin on the surface but in fact disguised a cavernous underground container.

She hurled the bag down into the bin, trying to throw her anger in along with it, attempting to prevent the old feelings of worthlessness from resurfacing from the dark pit she'd consigned them to.

Her chest heaved as she tried to get her breathing back under control. She slammed the lid shut but still the familiar anger buzzed through her veins. Rage rose like a fist inside her, grabbing her throat and squeezing it.

Not good enough. I'll never be good enough. Never...

She was going to be left behind again.

Always left behind. Never special enough to be wanted for good, like Holly and Sophie and Amelia and sodding everyone else.

Tash bit her lip hard, tasting salty blood. Her fingers curled into fists, her nails dug hard into her palms in an attempt to stop herself crying. She'd used the method countless times. When they'd told her mum was dead, when they'd told her that her foster sister Julie was being adopted but that Tash was being moved on to yet another foster family, when they said they'd couldn't locate her dad... Oh, so many times she'd needed something to stop her from crying in front of them, officials in uniforms, officials in suits...

The nail thing always worked, the physical pain in her palms concentrated her mind somehow, as though leaking a little of the emotional pain somehow stopped a full-on breach of the dam.

It was all too close to the surface lately with Sophie leaving, Holly pregnant, Amelia engaged. That left behind, never good enough feeling had been resurrected with a vengeance.

This thing with Nate had just knocked the lid off of it all. But as far as he was concerned she'd known this would never be a long-term thing, hadn't she? So why was she so bothered? He was only out here for a month and she was an easy source of sex for him, that was all. He hadn't even had to go out looking to get lucky.

She was convenient, that was all.

That's not all it is, it can't be.

Tash repressed the softer thoughts with as much, if not more savagery than she'd dealt with the cruel thoughts. She wasn't like Rebecca; she understood how the world worked. She was tough. She stood outside the chalet, her face tilted up to the sun with her eyes squeezed tightly, painfully shut.

"Tash."

At Holly's voice Tash snapped her eyes open, jumping.

"Oh. Hi," Tash replied but didn't meet Holly's eyes.

She'd been quiet coming back into Chalet Repos last night but there'd been no keeping Rebecca quiet about the fact Tash and Nate had disappeared together.

Everyone knew.

"Nice night out?" Holly raised an eyebrow.

"Not bad." Tash did meet Holly's gaze now. Holly looked pale, her eyes bloodshot and tired. "Do you mind?"

"No...but..." Holly frowned. "Be careful, yeah?"

Be careful of what? Getting hurt? Making a fool of myself? Ruining the potential deal between Scott and Nate?

"Sure, of course I will," Tash replied, faking nonchalance. "You know me."

"And you're...okay?" Holly asked, forehead crinkling.

"Yep, and you? How's the morning sickness today?" Tash headed into the chalet, knowing Holly wouldn't interrogate her in front of other people. It wasn't fair to dump all her problems on Holly, she had enough to deal with at the moment.

"Not great." Holly sighed. "Anyway I wanted to find you. It turns out we can't do the mountain cabin trip next week as Mr Campbell, er, Nate, needs to go to Geneva early on Monday."

"Oh?" Tash liked the idea of being in the cabin with Nate but of course there would be Rebecca and the others around too. That could be really awkward after what she'd overheard this morning.

"So I've spoken to Jake and Emily and they can take you on Friday instead." Holly followed her down the corridor.

"Are we all going to fit in the cabin?" Tash asked doubtfully.

"Jake's found a second cabin nearby and made arrangements with the farmer who owns it. Emily has promised to make sure it's habitable and clean."

"Oh?" Tash repeated. Her imagination went into overdrive, thinking about her and Nate, lying naked in front of a crackling fire in the wood-burner. But would Rebecca really be willing to leave them alone together?

Stop it. Stop thinking like this.

"You can tell me you know." Holly laid a hand on Tash's arm, the diamond on her ring finger flashing, seeming to taunt Tash. "If there's anything you need to talk about."

"I'm fine." The automatic response slipped out of Tash's mouth before she'd had time to think about it. "But thanks anyway."

She slipped away as quickly as she could, feeling distinctly odd. Her chest felt tight, the breath caught in her throat. The urge to talk to Holly, to tell her everything, burned inside her.

I don't do talking about the past. There's absolutely no point, it doesn't help anything. God knows they made me do it enough when I was growing up. Or tried to at least.

Talking about past events just brought it into the present. Repression was underrated. As a strategy it had kept Tash sane. As far as she was concerned life began at eighteen when she went travelling with her first sort-of boyfriend.

Went travelling and never stopped. Until now.

Tash bumped into Rebecca in the dorm room. Rebecca flashed her a wounded look, gleaming blonde ponytail swishing. Tash was reminded of an angry horse flicking its tail.

She sighed. There was so much going on in her head right now, she could do without this. She went to her locker for her make-up and then pulled out the rucksack stashed under Rebecca's bunk.

She packed the few things she'd need for the trip on Friday into her rucksack. Turning she noticed Rebecca still glaring at her.

"What's your problem Rebecca?" Tash sighed and sank down onto the floor cross-legged.

Might as well get this over with.

"You couldn't help yourself could you?" Rebecca scowled. "You knew I liked him."

"We're not teenagers Rebecca," Tash replied, exasperated. "You don't get first dibs on a man just because you say so. If you'd been in love with him for years or he was an ex of yours then fine, but we met him at the same time."

"But you can get pretty much any guy you want. It's easy for you, it's not easy for me," Rebecca hissed.

Everything else is pretty easy for you though, isn't it?

Tash took a deep breath. "I like him, a lot, okay? He's different and I kind of think it's up to him who he sees anyway."

"Why don't you like me Tash? Ever since I got here I've had the feeling you've got it in for me." Rebecca started to cry, big fat tears rolling down her perfectly tanned cheeks.

Tash stared at her, horrified, then she edged closer, awkwardly patting Rebecca on the leg. "Hey, I don't not like you. It's...complicated. I was really close to Sophie you know."

"It's hardly my fault I'm not Sophie." Rebecca sniffed and stared suspiciously, not mollified.

Oh crap, I'm going to have to give her more, really make her understand.

"If you want the truth I'm...well I'm...jealous of you," Tash admitted, sighing again. Today was turning into an emotional roller coaster.

"Why on earth would you be jealous of me?" Rebecca widened her eyes. "You're so popular."

I am?

Tash paused, a bizarre desire to tell Rebecca the truth squeezing the air out of her lungs, swelling inside her and making her throat constrict. She wanted to reassure Rebecca this was an issue that had nothing to do with her personally.

It was as though Nate had removed the stopper from her memories, broken some spell of silence and now she couldn't stop them tumbling out. The urge to tell the truth, to be understood, won out.

"You have a home back in England, a family who care about you, a safety net. I'll bet they paid for you to go to uni too?" Tash looked up at Rebecca.

Rebecca nodded. "Well yes...but..."

"You have a family, you've been protected by money," Tash cut her off, trying to speak calmly. Why did so many people with families never appreciate what they had? She had no patience for 'poor little rich girl' routines.

"I suppose," Rebecca replied quietly.

"Well I don't know if Holly has told you that I grew up in care?" Tash asked.

Rebecca shook her head.

Of course Holly wouldn't have told anyone.

"I...lost my family and I was brought up in foster homes, lots of them." Tash took the plunge, the urge to make Rebecca understand driving her ever deeper into the emotional quagmire.

"Oh?" Rebecca sniffed and stirred uneasily on her bunk but a spark of understanding in her eyes gave Tash the courage to continue. Just as well, as Tash wasn't sure she could stop now.

What does it matter? It's only words, just vibrations on the air. It means nothing really.

A familiar numbness crept over her as it always did when she was feeling too much. It allowed her to take a step back from herself. She stared at the bunk bed opposite, not sure what to say next.

"Couldn't you get adopted?"

Rebecca's innocent question felt like a body blow.

"More than anything I wanted a family, a proper home, to feel normal. But back when I was in the care system once you reached the age of nine, your adoption prospects were pretty much over.

Think about that, by ten you were finished. I wasn't especially cute, or all that well behaved. Plus I came with a lot of baggage." Tash stared down at the strap on her rucksack, unable to look at Rebecca now. She picked at a loose thread. "I've heard it's even worse now, once a child reaches six their chances of adoption go down the toilet."

"That's very sad," Rebecca replied.

"Yes, it is. Sad." Tash blinked hard. "Anyway, I'm sorry if I've made you feel...unwelcome here. I'm just going through a bad time at the moment. I do like you and I'm sorry if I let my...stuff affect our relationship. Shall we try and start again?"

Only now did she look back up at Rebecca, she flinched at the sympathy she found there but made herself keep looking, punishing herself.

"Of course," Rebecca said. "And I'm not surprised Nathaniel Campbell prefers you."

She sighed and Tash wasn't sure how to reply. She lightly patted Rebecca's denim clad knee. "You'll find someone, you're really pretty. And...nice. And you have really great hair. I'm jealous, I've always wanted swishy hair."

"Thanks." Rebecca smiled, self-consciously fingering her ponytail.

Who her parents are isn't her fault. And she is nice.

"Anyway," Tash added. "I bet I'm just a diversion for him, it's not like I'm going to be his girlfriend or anything."

Please disagree with me. Please.

"Hmm," Rebecca replied absent-mindedly, reaching into her bag for her Chanel compact and not commenting.

Tash's heart sank a little bit further.

Get real Tash, it means nothing. It's just sex, very good sex but sex nonetheless.

But it had felt like more. Sex didn't normally touch her in this way, or affect her this deeply. She remembered Nate kissing the scars on her arm and had to suppress the desire to lie on the floor and howl.

Was he thinking about her? Was it just a one off for him? Tash had chalked up her fair share of one-night stands but they had been different, they felt different. She wanted more of Nate. Not just sex but his attention, his focus. It made her feel...

Shaken. Stirred.

Like life was really full of possibilities, even for her.

That's tosh you know. Get real. You're a disposable shag, a nobody.

A familiar pain rose up in her, choking her, weighing her down. She closed her eyes briefly then rose and slipped into the bathroom, locking the door. She stood, resting her forehead on the cool mosaic wall tiles.

I am not a nobody.

The fierce rebuttal didn't soothe the pain. She didn't believe it. She'd been acting the part of the confident, chatty, bit of a laugh Tash for so long. But Tash was an invention. Natasha had been scared, miserable, desperate... Natasha had been swamped by pain, overwhelmed by it and convinced of her own worthlessness.

Dying her hair had given her confidence to act the part of a new 'her.' Being good at sex had been a tool to win popularity.

Who the hell am I?

She gritted her teeth, suppressing the urge to smash her forehead into the tiles. This was Nate's fault. If he hadn't noticed, hadn't prised the lid off her emotions she wouldn't be in this state.

If I'll never be good enough to be his girlfriend then I need to find some self-respect and refuse to be his convenient shag. I just... can't...cope with this.

She swung round and turned on the taps, splashing cold water over her face. She hadn't even noticed the tears sliding down her cheeks. Grabbing some loo roll she fiercely patted them away. She needed to repair her eye make up. Natasha might well be a mess but Tash didn't do getting dumped on. Nor did she do puffy red eyes.

Screw anyone who tries to put me down. Screw them all.

Chapter 6

Tash headed towards the kitchen; she needed a drink of water..

I don't do complicated...I haven't got time for complicated.

Nate's words echoed in Tash's head as she turned the corner only to bump into Greg.

"Madeleine is busy, can you take some coffee through to Nate?" He asked, typing into his Blackberry without even looking at her. "Only don't disturb him, he's working on his book and waiting for an important conference call. He hasn't got time to...chat."

Then he did look up, pushing his glasses further up his nose while his lips contorted into a smirk.

Patronising git.

"Message received loud and clear," Tash replied breezily, heading off to the kitchen before she lost her temper and said something she couldn't take back. She was certainly being tested this week.

Maybe he fancies Nate himself and is jealous?

Or perhaps he was warning her, being kind?

Yeah, right.

He hadn't sounded kind earlier, when he was talking to Madeleine. And there'd been nothing kind in his expression, it was gloating pure and simple. Well probably not pure but... Emotions swirled inside Tash, threatening to rise and burst the banks. While waiting for the coffee machine she glanced at the scars visible on her wrist. In some ways it felt like another lifetime when she'd been desperate enough to do that. Yet today the young Natasha felt very much alive and kicking inside her.

Mostly kicking.

She'd been kicking and hitting out for years, at anyone she felt deserved it. Now that behaviour felt immature and unsophisticated. Survival had been all she'd thought about for so long but what exactly was she surviving for? And when would she start living?

She bit her lip and carried the tray with coffee and cake to Nate's room, her heart pounding wildly and her chest tight again. Had last night meant anything to him? The morning after disconnected sex was awkward enough.

The morning after the kind of connected sex she'd had with Nate was hell.

She knocked on the door, expertly balancing the tray in one hand, hoping her make up effectively disguised her red-rimmed eyes.

He mustn't know I've been crying.

"Come in," Nate called.

When Tash entered he barely looked up, his eyes glued to his laptop screen.

"I've brought you coffee," Tash said, putting the tray down on the table.

"Thanks," Nate replied, still not looking up, frowning at his screen.

So that was how it was. Box labelled 'sex' now shut up and filed while the 'work' box had been opened. He was busy, important... she got that, really she did but today it felt like someone had lit the fuse to a box of fireworks inside her and she'd kill for a hug, for any kind of assurance that she wasn't disposable trash.

I don't do complicated...

Nate's words taunted her again. There was no way round it, she knew she was more complicated than the *Times*' crossword and

72

the Sudoku puzzles Lucy loved all rolled into one.

"So it's, erm, going well?" She couldn't seem to leave it. She needed something from him.

Just leave the tray and walk away. Take your dignity with you. You need to act cool. Remember he's bad for you.

He shot her coping strategies to pieces. Remembering that had to give her the strength to turn him down if he did want a repeat performance.

"Yes, fine thanks," Nate replied distractedly. "Sorry, I'm expecting a call, was there anything else?"

He finally looked up at met her eyes. The flash of connection she found there startled her again.

"What's wrong?" He sighed, rubbing at his forehead and with that sigh Tash felt her last hopes ebbing away.

She was a nuisance and bothering him, that much was obvious. What could she say anyway? 'Your staff were nasty to me'. Hardly. Telling tales would make her look petty.

As to what was really wrong? Well it felt too deep for words, too complicated to be encapsulated in one sentence or two. And it was clear he barely had time for even that.

"Nothing's wrong." She gritted her teeth. "Well, I'll probably see you later then."

"Great, see you later." Nate smiled briefly but then looked back to his laptop again, Tash seemingly forgotten.

She turned to leave the room feeling dismissed and very, very small.

It's all my own fault. What was I expecting exactly?

And what would she do with herself now? She wasn't in the mood to ski.

Get drunk.

Tash knew she had a couple of hours free, not enough to ski really, it wasn't worth the hassle and she wasn't in the mood.

Sophie, I need to speak to Sophie.

Holly felt out of bounds at the moment, distracted and stressed.

Tash didn't want to add to that. But Sophie was always reliable and she'd just got engaged so she was probably floating, nothing Tash confided in her could bring her down.

Tash headed for the Bar des Amis. She didn't bother with a coat again. She'd doubtless regret it later when the sun sank down behind the Dents du Midi mountain range and the temperature plummeted but she couldn't bring herself to care.

Nate filled her thoughts. With every step she remembered how he'd felt inside her, how he'd teased her body, playing her with expert ease. But it was the memory of him kissing the scars on her arm that threw her the most and threatened to break her resolve to keep him at a distance.

I don't do complicated.

Tash increased her pace, her boots pounding angrily into the compacted snow not yet cleared from the pavements.

It's not my bloody fault. I didn't ask for the things that have made me complicated.

Hot tears pricked at her eyes.

Christ, now I'm leaking again.

This wouldn't do. What on earth was happening to her? Nate had ripped her open and left her raw and exposed while he got on with building his business empire. No doubt his book was going to be about how wonderful he was and that everyone should be like him.

You're not being fair to him. He never promised you anything. Quite the opposite in fact.

Tash ground her teeth. Life wasn't fucking fair so why did she have to be? And he hadn't kept up his side of the bargain. Everyone knew no strings sex wasn't supposed to be emotional. He'd been the one to detonate the bomb and change the rules, not her.

Say she did spend the next month having sex with Nate, how was she going to cope when he dumped her and did a bunk back to London?

Anger pulsed through her veins and rose up in her throat like bile. When she tried to swallow it back down the pain festered inside her, steam building as though she were a pressure cooker coming up to the boil.

She paused, looking over the barrier next to the road, down the steep drop to the valley below. The barrier could easily be climbed over. If she fell down the mountainside to the rocks below it would all be over. Quickly.

Stop it, stop it. I won't...I'm never going down that route again.

Tash bit the inside of her lip hard, tasting blood on her tongue. Memories she'd stowed away came unbidden to her mind. She remembered the first time she'd tried to kill herself, when she was thirteen years old. She'd taken an overdose, convinced in some warped teenage way she was fated to die like her mother.

She could picture the faded floral wallpaper in the small box room of her foster family's house, feel the despair that had washed over her as she swallowed pill after pill. Not a cry for help. What was the point of that? She had nothing but the state's idea of help and ironically it hadn't helped one bit.

She actually wanted to die. And there'd been that doctor at A & E who'd treated her like a toddler who'd swallowed tablets thinking they were Smarties. She could still picture that doctor now with her long dark hair pulled back, thick-rimmed spectacles and a patronising expression.

"You could have done some serious damage to yourself," she'd said.

That had actually been the point.

The supposed 'help' she'd received at the adolescent unit while being assessed had sort of helped but certainly not in the way they'd intended. It'd been there she learnt to cut herself from the other patients. All of the girls were at it and some of the boys. Not one doctor or social worker ever picked up on it. It had certainly reinforced her opinion that adults were stupid and not to be trusted.

Cutting had helped, in a way. A method of controlling the pain, of coping with the anger.

With effort she jerked herself out of the memory. This was all Nate's fault. She was doing fine before he came along. Well maybe not 'fine' exactly but she hadn't had suicidal thoughts or cut herself in years.

Suicidal.

The word echoed in her mind, sending a chill down her spine. It was the ultimate rebellion against life itself. It was the final 'fuck you' to the world.

It was part of her past. She wasn't suicidal now, just remembering the feeling from years ago. There was a big difference.

Tash gulped huge lungfuls of mountain air and crossed to the other side of the road, away from the steep drop, as though afraid her body might act of its own accord.

I have to stop this thing with Nate or I might completely lose it.

If this was how she felt about the prospect of losing Nate after just one night with him then what on earth would it be like after an affair lasting a whole month?

She pushed away the instinctive desire that rose instantly at the idea of a month's sex with Nate. Next time, if there was a next time, she had to resist, however difficult it was. Fear clutched at her chest as she realised how close she'd been to the edge back there. The solution was obvious. Any rejection triggered terrible feelings in Tash so she had to employ her age-old technique of avoiding rejection - reject them before they get the chance to reject you.

It was simple but effective as a defensive measure.

A pang of disappointment at the decision briefly flickered inside her.

Tough.

She couldn't waver, it would be too dangerous...

Finally she reached the Bar des Amis, pausing outside the sign-written plate glass window to look in. It was fairly empty, the lunchtime rush was over, and Sophie sat at a table with Amelia. Tash hovered as she'd wanted Sophie to herself this afternoon. Then she noticed the wedding magazines on the table.

A strange coldness crept over Tash and she backed away, but not before Sophie had looked up and noticed her.

Sophie walked quickly to the door and came out. Luc's dog Max ran out first, jumping up excitedly at Tash. She usually brought him left over sausages from breakfast when she came by.

"Nothing today Maxie boy, sorry." Tash scratched him on the head and stroked his velvety ears, thinking it might be nice to have the kind of lifestyle where she could have a dog. She'd never had a pet. Not even a rabbit...

Sophie hurried towards Tash, her smile faltering when she saw Tash's smudged eye make-up.

"Come here you," Sophie said softly, her tone so full of love Tash struggled not to burst into tears there and then. She guessed Sophie was talking to her and not to the dog. She hoped so anyway.

Tash walked towards her and let Sophie envelope her in a big hug.

"Hey you," Sophie whispered into Tash's ear.

"H...hi," Tash replied, burying her face into Sophie's hair, inhaling the familiar scent of her apricot scented shampoo and freshly washed hair.

A sense of comfort washed over her.

"Do you want to come and join me and Amelia for a coffee?" Sophie asked.

"Not really," Tash whispered, her voice shaky. "I miss you Sophie."

"I miss you too." Sophie hugged her even tighter.

"You know if we stand like this for much longer people will start spreading rumours about us. They'll say we're lovers," Tash joked to break the intensity of the moment.

"Puerile idiots, let people think what they like. I couldn't care less what goes on in their filthy little minds," Sophie answered. "You needed a hug."

"I did," Tash agreed.

"Can you come over this evening?" Sophie fished in her jeans' pocket and brought out a clean tissue which she handed to Tash. She smiled sympathetically. "You know you can come over any time, don't you? You're always welcome."

"Thanks," Tash muttered and wiped her eyes with the tissue. The tide of emotion had receded inside her. Threat over. Peace soothing the savagery, taming it.

For now.

"You know what, I think I will join you," Tash said. "But I'd rather have a proper drink."

I need to be with friends. I also need to get very drunk if said friends are doing wedding talk.

Nate sat back in his chair and hit save on his Word document. He was pleased with himself. In spite of the conference call he'd managed four thousand words, the autocorrect sorting out all the mistakes his dyslexic brain had made.

If only I'd had this when I was younger. At school.

His teachers would never have believed he would go on to write a book. They hadn't been great at dealing with the problem, his dyslexia hadn't been recognised until he was in his late teens. When he'd recently spoken to a group of teachers he'd been assured it would have been a different picture if he'd been born twenty years later.

But he hadn't. He'd struggled and become the class joker to cover up the fact he was struggling. It had been easy to fall in with the wrong crowd. If it hadn't been for what happened to his mate Matthew when they were seventeen who knew where he might have ended up?

You'll never amount to anything.

How many times had he heard that phrase? Teachers held such power. Some were great but others...well he sometimes wondered if they'd seen his television programme and remembered teaching him, belittling him...

All the more reason to get this book right.

It mattered.

Who knew who might read it and understand that whatever had happened to them so far, there was always hope they could turn their lives around? Nobody had to be defined by their problems. He met so many bright young people who had something to contribute to the world but had derailed somewhere along the way. All he tried to do was give them the chance to get back on track again. The rest was always up to them.

He'd asked permission to put some of their stories into the book, changing the names of course, usually to protect the guilty rather than the innocent though. Some adults were spectacularly skilled at screwing children up.

He shut down his laptop and his thoughts strayed back to Tash again. She was so achingly vulnerable. He'd been caught up in getting his chapter ending right when she'd brought him coffee. Maybe he should have stopped and paid her some attention. But the blank Word document had been taunting him for weeks and today the words had finally been flowing, pouring out of him at such speed his fingers could barely keep up. He hadn't wanted to stop in case the flow didn't come back again.

She'll understand, surely, she knows I'm busy. And she was the one who skipped out last night.

He'd make it up to her at the weekend. The mountain cabin idea sounded like fun and Rebecca had already spoken to him, suggesting he and Tash take the smaller cabin while she took Madeleine, Greg and Robert to the other larger hut. Getting a fire going and sharing a sleeping bag with Tash sounded like the perfect way to spend the night. He'd make love to her slowly, kissing every inch of her body. He grew hard just thinking about it.

Make love.

That was odd, it wasn't a phrase he usually applied to sex. In fact he wasn't sure he'd ever used it.

I want to show Tash just how special she is. She needs to know.

Yet this wasn't going to go anywhere; how could it? And could he be doing more harm than good? He had undeniable feelings for her. Quite what they were he wasn't sure yet. But he knew he wanted to get to know her, that spending time with her somehow reminded him of who he really was. She grounded him.

Words were not his area of expertise, despite today's word count. Had he upset her earlier? He'd earned some time off, he'd go see if he could find her.

He bumped into Holly in the hallway.

"Any idea where I'll find Tash?"

She stared at him for a moment as though trying to read his face. How much did she know?

Eventually she answered him. "If she is not in the chalet she's probably at Bar des Amis in town, it's owned by friends of ours. Here, I'll show you where it is on the map."

She opened up a maps app on her phone and showed him.

"Okay, thanks." He memorised it and headed towards his jacket and boots.

He had a feeling she wanted to say more but after Madeleine this morning he'd had his fill of unsolicited advice.

When he stepped outside, the chill mountain air hit him. The temperature dropped rapidly as he walked. Luckily he quickly reached the Bar des Amis. Tash was sitting at the bar on her own, talking to a girl behind the bar.

He walked up to her and, without asking, slipped onto a stool next to her.

"Hi," he said to Tash, then turned to smile at the girl behind the bar. "You're English?"

It was a safe assumption as he'd never seen such a pure English rose complexion.

"Yes, my fiancé is Swiss though. I'm Sophie. What can I get you?"

"Do you do coffee? I could do with warming up, the walk here was pretty chilly." He turned to Tash. "Can I get you anything Tash?"

Sophie's eyebrows rose and the corners of her lips twitched into a small smile.

"Vodka and coke please," Tash replied without looking at him.

Is she still pissed off with me?

Sophie hesitated, concern flickering in her eyes.

"Okay, but take it easy Tash, right?" Sophie turned to sort out the drinks.

So Sophie is worried about Tash drinking? Interesting.

"I like this place," he said, his tone casual, pretending he hadn't noticed Tash was ignoring him.

The bar had the kind of laid-back vibe of the pubs he used to go to, before life got too hectic. Although the cowhide covered barstools and the old-fashioned ski photos might have looked out of place in a London pub. It was the polar opposite to The Living Room at the W but he liked it.

"Oh, you've got time to talk to me now have you?" Tash sniped.

She is pissed off.

"I get...single-minded about things when I'm working." He pulled a face. "It's nothing personal, it's just the way I am, I've always had tunnel vision. And writing a book is something new for me. A bit of a challenge."

She turned towards him. He detected a slight thaw in her facial expression.

"Oh?" She took the drink Sophie put in front of her and sipped at it.

"Yes. My old English teacher Miss Pringle would have a fit if she knew I was writing a book."

"Why?" Tash fingered the moisture on the outside of her glass.

Definitely thawing. I may even get a whole sentence out of her next if I'm lucky.

"I'm dyslexic. Didn't know it back then. I used to muck around in class a lot to stop people noticing I was struggling."

"I can relate to that," Tash said, looking him in the eye finally.

I guess you can. I think you're probably an expert at the smokescreen.

"Your coffee." Sophie put a cup in front of him on the bar. Nate broke eye contact with Tash. "Thanks."

"So, how is the book going?" Tash asked, turning slightly towards Nate on her stool.

"It's going a bit better today than it was yesterday," he admitted. "I was finally getting some words down, that's why I shut you out earlier."

"Oh, I see." She sipped at her drink again.

"Do you always drink this early?" He asked.

She rolled her eyes at him. "Do you always tell people what to do?"

"Pretty much," he said, smiling at her. "I've made a living out of it."

She laughed and relief surged through him.

Why do I care so much what she thinks of me?

"Why are you writing the book?" She asked, her catlike eyes displaying a genuine spark of curiosity.

"I want to inspire people," he replied simply. "To make them believe they can change their lives."

"So, what inspired you then?"

Shall I give her the sanitised version from my bio? Or...

He wanted to share things with her. Wanted to reconnect with her.

"Well, I told you I used to mess about a lot at school..."

"Behind the bike sheds?" she asked.

"Yep, behind the bike sheds, in the classroom, wherever really." He kept his tone serious. "So, I got into quite a bit of trouble. That all changed the night my best mate Matthew decided to nick a car and ended up totalling it, rolling down an embankment. I was in the back and I got off with a broken shoulder and a few bruises. Matthew was dead on impact. My other friend Paul was in the passenger seat and he ended up in a wheelchair."

Tash stared at him, transfixed. She'd twisted round so now she was facing him, her knee touching his.

"Oh god, that's awful. I'm sorry," she said, placing one of her hands over his.

"You asked what inspired me to change my life. That was it, realising I was throwing it away." Nate exhaled. "Then I discovered there were ways you could succeed and make money without passing exams. Luckily I was good with numbers. I suppose that's why this book matters so much to me. Not just to show Miss Pringle, although I am thinking of sending her a signed copy."

Tash laughed. "I can see how that would be satisfying."

"I want people to see that no matter what life has dealt them they can find a way to turn things around, get back on track. Sometimes all someone needs is a little help. There's no shame in it. We all need a helping hand occasionally."

Tash picked up her drink again, her expression wistful as she raised a glass to her lips. Something told him she got why his book mattered more than most people. More than Madeleine or Greg or Rob ever could.

Tash wasn't a distraction from his book, she was a reminder of why he needed to get it right. Plus being here helped him to remember who he really was, the man before fame had turned things a little crazy.

"So, why are you in here, drinking on your own?" he asked.

Tash looked away. "I wasn't on my own, I was with Sophie and Amelia until recently. They were looking at wedding magazines."

The face she pulled it would have been comical if he hadn't glimpsed the flicker of naked pain, quickly masked by the grimace.

"I guess that would be enough to drive someone to drink," he said.

He also guessed Tash was used to using alcohol to mask her emotions.

This time it was his turn to put a hand on top of hers.

"I just feel a little left behind. Like everyone else has got their lives sorted out and I...haven't." Tash bit her lip.

"Oh, the magic 'everyone ,'" he said. "People usually feel a hell of a lot less sorted than the image they project to the rest of the

83

world."

"Even you?" She snorted. "You're sorted, surely?"

"Maybe not so much as you think," he said. "You know I lost all my money when I was twenty-four?"

"Really?"

"Yes, I lost my first company." He shrugged. "You'd be surprised how many successful entrepreneurs have actually lost everything and been pretty successful failures at one time or another."

"That surprises me."

"The difference is we wallow for maybe a day or two and then we get off our arses and make it all back again."

"Just like that?"

"It's hard work, I'm not saying it isn't," Nate paused. "I suppose what I'm trying to say is that things can change. We can change them. I've got lots of case studies I'm using in my book that prove it."

Tash really wanted it to be true. She stared down at Nate's hand on hers.

"Everything changes," he added. "The question is whether you want things to happen to you or you want to be the one making things happen."

"Things do seem to be happening to me recently," Tash said, her mind racing.

"So, you need to think about what you want out of life and work out how you're going to get it," Nate said.

Damn good intentions, who needed them?

I want you.

How could she ignore the desire pulsing through her body? She wanted Nate, needed him to help her push away the pain. She licked her lips and placed her other hand on his knee.

"I can think of something I'd like right now." She put as much emphasis into her words and smile as she could.

"I'm not sure if that's such a good idea," Nate said.

It felt like he'd slapped her. She physically recoiled in shock,

84

yanking her hand out from beneath his and her other hand off his knee. Then she slipped from her bar stool, unsteady on her feet.

Stupid, stupid, stupid girl.

"Tash," Nate called her name but she fled to the exit, not looking back.

She stepped outside and the freezing air assaulted her. She didn't care. She welcomed the numbing cold, hoping it could numb her completely.

Wrapping her arms around her body, she stood still for a moment, indecision freezing her as much as the temperature.

Where do I go now?

Horrid, familiar bleakness crept over her like a shroud.

This is where I always end up – rejected. On my own. It's why I decided never to put myself in these situations.

Stupid, stupid, stupid girl.

It felt like a trapdoor had opened and she was falling.

I wasn't even worth a second go.

She whimpered, desperately trying to swallow back the pain, the humiliation throbbing through her body.

"Tash, wait." Nate put his hand on her arm and she shook it free.

Snowflakes began to fall from the darkening sky, growing increasingly thicker. They landed on Tash's hair and stung her cheeks.

"Will you please let me explain?" Nate glanced up at the snow-laden sky as though he'd only just noticing it was snowing.

"It's fine, there's nothing to explain." Tash stamped her feet on the impacted snow at the edge of the pavement.

"There is. Look you're freezing, put my jacket on and wait here while I go back in and pay. Then we can walk back together."

Nate draped his jacket over her shoulders and headed back inside. Tash waited until he was out of sight and then she set off, walking briskly and taking a detour so he wouldn't find her on the obvious route back to Chalet Repos.

Why did I proposition him? Why? When will I learn?

It was simple – don't form attachments and don't open yourself up to rejection. It had worked for her so far. Living with Holly and Sophie had made her soft. Well, he needn't think she was going to humiliate herself again. She'd been stupid to share. Stupid to imagine she was good enough for Nate.

Stupid, stupid, stupid girl.

Nate's jacket carried his scent. It brought back memories of him kissing her neck, him making love to her. She pulled it tighter around her body. As she walked through Verbier, not caring or knowing she was going, silent tears ran down her cheeks.

This wasn't going to break her. She'd survived worse. Much worse. She just had to toughen up again. There would be other warm beds to share.

She squashed down an inner protest that she didn't want other men.

I will survive this. And Nate can go take a flying leap into a snowdrift.

Nate supposed he shouldn't have been surprised that Tash had run out on him for a second time before he'd had a chance to explain. It seemed to be a bit of a habit of hers. He'd looked for her but hadn't been able to find any trace. Eventually he'd been forced back to Chalet Repos by the cold, comforted that at least she had his jacket on.

Blast the girl, couldn't she have waited two minutes? But deep down he understood. She was like a wounded animal, terrified to trust, biting out at any rescuers in a desperate attempt to protect itself.

He hadn't seen her at the chalet the next day, though he had checked she got home safely. In her absence he'd been trying to get as many words down as possible. Then yesterday he had seen her but there'd always been other people around. She'd blanked him at dinner, refusing to meet his eyes.

Now he was supposed to be going to some remote mountain

cabin with her. Maybe this meant he'd actually get a chance to talk to her.

I've got a decision to make.

Nate stared into the flames of the fire, abandoning the attempt to read through what he'd written earlier on his iPad.

He wanted Tash, no question. But she was damaged, vulnerable. A month long fling ran the risk of hurting her even more. If it was just about sex maybe he could walk away but there was this persistent sense of connection, the surprise appearance of genuine feelings for her.

Feelings that had stopped him saying 'yes' to her offer in the bar. If he was going to make love to her again he had to be sure they both wanted more than the kind of fling that could only damage her more.

Because this connection between them could become something...more. Something special.

That could be difficult if she refused to talk to him.

"Everything okay?" Scott's voice broke through Nate's thoughts.

"Yeah, sure." Nate blinked and smiled. "Just chilling."

"So, you're enjoying Verbier so far?" Scott asked.

"Definitely." Nate tried to turn his thoughts back to business. "I agree with you that now is a prime time for investment, particularly with everything that's going into the mountain biking trails. It makes it a more year-round proposition."

Scott face relaxed. "And you're getting on okay with Tash... and Rebecca?"

Rebecca had clearly been an afterthought. Scott's way of being polite.

"Tash has been looking after me, yes." Nate knew that the double meaning of his words would not be lost on Scott.

"She's a great girl," Scott said . "A very loyal friend and worker. In that order."

"But fragile?" Nate asked.

Scott stared thoughtfully into the fire, considering the question.

"Tash is tough. She's strong. Don't mistake her vulnerability for weakness. Um, probably too much information, sorry. It's not for me to get involved."

"As we're getting personal - when did you know that Holly was right for you?" Nate asked.

Scott looked surprised. "Well, that would be when she took a client's bra out from under her sweater. Long story, you had to be there. The thing is, I think you know fairly soon, on a deeper level, it just takes your mind a while to catch up."

Nate stared back into the fire. That made sense. For all his soul-searching, there was an insistent drum beating deep inside him, telling him Tash was the girl for him.

She helps me to remember the real me.

With everything that came with the TV series and the trappings of success and money it was easy to slip into his public persona. People expected him to be exactly how he was on the TV show. All the time. He was never allowed to be in a bad mood or to have an off day. He'd got used to it, or thought he had. But far from distracting him, Tash had reminded him what was really important.

And I don't give a toss what Madeleine or anyone else thinks. I've never cared what other people think so why start now?

He needed to talk to Tash. He was going to make sure she listened to him if he had to pin her down or tie her up again so that she couldn't run away until he'd had his say.

Chapter 7

"I've arranged it so you can be alone with Nathaniel tonight," Rebecca said, beaming, clearly expecting Tash's undying gratitude.

"You have?" Tash widened her eyes, heart pounding hard. She shouldn't be surprised. The fact she'd been avoiding Nate and ignoring him in public would only convince the others that they were at it like rabbits.

She didn't know how she felt about being alone with him at the mountain cabin. Part of her desperately wanted to be with him again, to recapture the intimacy she'd experienced with him at Bar des Amis, to glimpse the optimism and sense anything might be possible again.

Sure, he has the power to lift you up. But he also has the power to smash you into tiny pieces.

"Yes." Rebecca smiled. "I was being...immature and I'm sorry, really I am."

Tash smiled awkwardly back, trying hard to focus on Rebecca and ignore the emotional maelstrom inside her. "I'm sorry too. Thank you for arranging things but I'm not sure...not sure...um."

She felt too ashamed to admit Nate had knocked her back the last time he had the opportunity.

Rebecca stepped forward and gave Tash a quick hug, startling her. They'd never hugged before.

She feels sorry for me.

This was one of the very good reasons why she never shared her story. Pity embarrassed her and she didn't want it. But Rebecca was making an effort and this wasn't the time to be difficult. She hugged Rebecca back, engulfed by her perfume.

Chanel no 5, of course.

Maybe Rebecca now had her eye on Greg or Robert. Tash's protective antenna twitched but she bit back her instincts to say anything. It was Rebecca's life. She'd be her friend, be there if she needed someone to talk to.

Like Sophie had been for her.

At the moment she had a much scarier conversation to face.

Nate smiled when they met at the Ski-Doos. She stared down at the snow.

She shouldn't have run out on him. It was immature. The past few days had given her time to think. She hadn't had any alcohol and hadn't been out except to ski.

Things were changing and throwing a tantrum wasn't going to stop them. It was time to find a way forward. Maybe she could ask Holly and Scott for more responsibility. They were moving out so perhaps she could volunteer to oversee Chalet Repos?

Nate had at least got her thinking. And he had a right turn her down if he wanted to.

Okay, she wasn't really okay with that last bit but she knew she ought to be. That had to count for something, surely?

She ended up sitting behind Nate on the Ski-Doo, arms around his waist. The noise of the engine made conversation difficult so she tried to rehearse what she needed to say to him, her heart beating so hard she was sure he must be able to feel it.

When they got to the hut, Tash let go of Nate reluctantly and slid off the Ski-Doo into the pristine, deep snow. She barely heard Emily and Jake's speech to the group about what they should do in an emergency.

Just being alone with Nate felt pretty catastrophic. Falling sick or keeping warm in bad weather conditions hardly registered in comparison. Rebecca's knowing smirk and Madeleine's disapproving stare as they split up barely registered either.

I feel sick.

When the group moved off she couldn't look at Nate. She grabbed her bedroll and bag and made her way into the hut, her heart still pounding. She began assembling firelighters and kindling in the stove. Anything to avoid looking at him.

"Hey, let me do that." Nate crouched down next to her and touched her elbow.

"It's okay," Tash mumbled, staring down.

"No, something's not okay," Nate replied calmly. "Okay, we'll get the fire going but then you and I are going to have a talk. If you try to run away again I warn you I'll track you down and bring you back over my shoulder if I have to. I'll go get the logs."

Tash rocked back on the heels of her boots as Nate left the hut, almost tempted to run to see if he'd actually do it.

The image of him doing just that flashed into her mind. Sexual desire flickered inside her, consuming her.

I can't do this. But I have to.

Once the fire had been lit and they'd unpacked their bedrolls and sleeping bags Tash summoned the courage to break the silence.

"I'm sorry I ran out on you at the bar." She stared at the flames licking the logs and remembered how it had felt to have his tongue on her skin.

Cherished, and so alive. Gloriously alive. Happy.

She struggled to understand why it couldn't happen again, her self-protective instincts competing with the sexual desire and an overwhelming visceral longing which was flooding her body.

She bit her lip, conflicting thoughts warring in her mind, unable to look at him.

Unable to breathe.

"You didn't give me a chance to explain why I didn't think sleeping together was a good idea the other night." Nate's voice was steady, calming her.

"No, I didn't but it's okay." Tash tried to keep her tone light. "You didn't want to, that's your choice."

"I never said I didn't want to," Nate said.

She turned towards him then, meeting his piercing stare. Her heartbeat picked up again, her skin prickled. She didn't want to believe it, didn't want to let her spirits rise in case he didn't mean it.

Even if he does want to sleep with you again you know he shouldn't. How are you going to feel when he sods off back to London?

"Then why..." she stared at him, trying to read him, not wanting to humiliate herself again.

"Why did I turn you down?" He asked.

"Yes," she said, forcing herself to remember to breathe.

"I think it's very easy to use drink or sex as a way of avoiding dealing with difficult emotions. I could tell you weren't okay that day and it felt like sleeping with me was just your way of shutting down."

"I see." She wanted to look away but forced herself to keep facing him. "It might have been...a little bit, that day. And I used to do that a lot but...it feels different with you. Like I'm remembering myself, not forgetting myself which it usually feels like, you know?"

"Yes, I think I do," he replied. "And just because I didn't think it was a good idea the other night doesn't mean that I don't think it's right another time."

Tash's breath caught at the top of her chest.

"I enjoyed talking to you the other evening. I like being with you, Tash." Nate's voice was low, he edged closer so their sides were touching. The firelight filled the small wooden hut with an amber glow, the warmth mellowing Tash, softening her resolve.

I'm lost. I can't shut him out. Can't say no.

She turned to look at him, pleading with her eyes, desperate for him to understand...to help her. He felt like a man who might actually have the map she needed to move on. He was certainly the only man she'd ever met who'd noticed her scars, who'd noticed her - the girl beneath the pink striped hair and loud behaviour, the Natasha buried deep inside her. The only one who'd made her feel there might be more for her in life.

She looked into his eyes, the connection she found there healing her, calming her down. Inspiring hope in her. He really believed in the stuff he preached. Maybe it wasn't too late for her and she could finally stop running away.

She had Sophie and Holly and the other girls too. They were her new family. If Nate walked away or broke her heart she'd survive, but a part of her dared to hope.

Will I get my happy ending too?

"I...I'm not sure." She leaned against his comforting bulk, heart pounding wildly in her chest, feeling a little dizzy.

"I like you Tash." Nate replied carefully. "I like you a lot. I think there is something special between us, something different. Something worth pursuing.."

"Oh?"

She squeezed her eyes tight shut, her previous certainties now elusive, scattered by Nate's words.

"I just want to say one thing. Isn't it time to stop rejecting people before they get the opportunity to reject you?" Nate asked. "Or am I going to have to invest in some running shoes?"

Tash jerked in surprise and turned to stare at him.

"What?" He raised an eyebrow. "You thought you were the only one who did that?"

Of course she knew that was what she did, she did possess some self-awareness. But she'd been doing it for so long it had become an instinctive part of her.

"Well it works." She shrugged.

How do you know me so well?

Yet it felt like they did know each other. When she looked into his eyes it seemed like they'd known each other forever, like they were finding each other again, however crazy that sounded. And it felt like someone turned the dial up on reality. Everything felt 'more.' Better, brighter, sharper.

Intensely alive.

How could she turn her back on this? Something told her you only got one Nate per lifetime.

Sophie would kill herself laughing if she could hear me. Who knew? I'm a romantic after all.

"Works...how exactly?" Nate's eyes shone as he leant forward, his neck so close she could smell citrus aftershave and his own unique scent. The scent that comforted her that night she ran off with his jacket and stopped her doing anything stupid. Somehow it had felt like he was with her.

Desire rose up inside her, throbbing between her legs and in her breasts, her body rebelling against her mind,

I've had enough meaningless sex to fill two lifetimes. I've had enough of never being considered special enough to be a proper girlfriend.

The thought stung her into taking a step back. "It stops me getting hurt."

"Does it?" He asked, softening his tone. "Really?"

He reached out to take one of her hands. She stared at his large hand wrapped around her own slender fingers.

Is he dependable? A safe pair of hands? Someone I can trust?

A sob burst out of her mouth before she could choke the pain back down. Nate stroked her hand.

"I do get that you needed to do it when you were younger. The care system can be brutal, I do know."

She laughed bitterly. "Oh really? Do you?"

In reply he lifted her hand to his mouth and kissed her palm tenderly, eyes fixed on her, not flinching from her pain.

"So tell me," he said. "Tell me what it was like."

"Do you know what it's like to be eight years old and rejected for adoption because you're getting too old to be cute and malleable?" Tash asked numbly. "Do you know what it's like to be rejected for having too much baggage? It's baggage I never even asked for, I had no control over it. I couldn't help having nightmares."

She wouldn't tell him about wetting the bed, she could feel the shame even now, of the wet nightclothes and the look of irritation on so many faces, even though some were nice and tried to hide their annoyance at the extra washing.

Every irritated look was another brick in the wall she erected around herself, shutting them out. Only too late did she realise that in keeping them at bay she had walled herself in. A prison of her own making.

"And now it's happening again, isn't it?" Tash felt silent tears coursing down her cheeks. "You might want to have sex with me but you'd never want someone like me as your girlfriend because you don't do complicated. It's okay, you did tell me upfront. It's not your fault...but... I can't help being really, really pissed off about it."

"What baggage?" Nate pulled her over so she was sitting half on his lap, cradled by his arms. "Tell me."

I want to feel safe, I want to relax, but how can I trust it? How can I trust him?

She would've preferred an argument with him. Anger was so much easier to deal with than pain.

But then she'd been using anger her whole life and she was sick of it. Sick of always being the bolshy one.

"When I told you I was sibling free I was only telling you half the truth. I did have a sister, a baby sister, Eva." Tash stared into the fire, watching the flames devouring the logs. "She died. Cot death."

"I'm really sorry to hear that." Nate stroked Tash's hair and a few of her muscles unclenched enough to allow her to relax into him. The warm bulk of him was comforting.

It felt safe here, in the middle of nowhere, in this tiny hut with nothing but herself and Nate. A safe place to let out her secrets, like lancing a wound.

Letting go.

"Mum and Dad stopped talking to each other and it was like they forgot I existed. They were fenced in by this huge sadness and

I couldn't reach them. It felt like I hadn't just lost a baby sister, I'd lost everything." Tash burrowed deeper into Nate's embrace. "But then I really did lose everything. Dad walked out because he just couldn't deal with it. Then Mum...well...she opted out. Permanently. Killed herself. While I was at school. When she didn't come to pick me up that day they called social services. Clearly I wasn't worth sticking around for or staying alive for."

The surge of intense pain racked her body and she sobbed into him for a while. When the sobs were under control Nate cleared his throat.

"Didn't social services track your dad down after your mum died?" he asked.

"No, they tried," Tash replied, feeling numb, washed out by the waves of pain she'd held back for so long. "They think he went to Australia."

"What about relatives?"

"My dad had fallen out with his family and Mum was an only child. I did have a gran but she'd had a stroke the year before and had moved into sheltered housing. I can see things more clearly now I'm older. I know Mum was suffering from depression, she'd had bad post natal depression after Eva was born. Also I think Gran probably did want me but she wasn't allowed. But when you're eight you don't see things clearly. All I knew then was no one wanted me and I must be really unlovable if even my own parents didn't love me."

Tash bit her lip. She wanted to curl her nails into her palms to control the pain but Nate held both her hands too firmly for her to pull away.

"How did you cope with it?" he asked.

"I stopped talking. I refused to cooperate with anyone, became a bit of a rebel."

"Really? I can't imagine that." Nate said, the corners of his lips twitching.

Tash smiled with him. It felt odd, smiling, when what they were talking about was so awful but Nate somehow made it all feel less terrible. Certainly better than having it all locked up inside her.

"Some of the foster homes were okay," she added. "But when I realised no one wanted to keep me permanently, I acted up. I felt so unbelievably angry. All the time. It got me nowhere though and I was just passed around the system, rejected over and over again. It was catch twenty-two, I acted up because no one wanted me and pretty soon no one wanted me because I acted up."

Tash looked up at Nate, the understanding she saw in his eyes comforted her.

"I'm sorry, I must be boring you with all this, and this trip is supposed to be a work project so if you want me to shut up..." She bit her lip again, ready to shut down again, watching him closely and listening for any nuance in his tone that might indicate he wanted to recoil from her and her pain.

Please don't say yes, please want to know...

"Tash." Nate narrowed his eyes. "You know the saying 'don't ask a question you don't want the answer to?' Well I never ask anything I don't want to know. It's important, all this stuff, particularly if you've never really talked about it."

"I thought your philosophy was all about forgetting your past, not using it as an excuse." She stared down at their entwined hands.

"Yes, but sometimes the only way to get over your past is to confront it. Bring it out in the open, deal with it and *then* move on." Nate asserted confidently.

"You make it sound so easy." Tash snorted. "Hey, no one loved me but never mind eh?"

"Idiot," Nate chided. "You know that's not what I meant. And I never said it was easy."

Then he kissed her, lips covering hers with exquisite tenderness but before it could morph into a foreplay kiss he pulled back.

"That was nice, come back." Tash moved her face closer, lips parted.

"Talk first, sex second," he said sternly.

"You are so strict." she pretend pouted.

It felt great to be teasing again, as though maybe the world wasn't about to cave in on her after all.

"Do you want me to put you over my knee?" Nate quirked a thick eyebrow.

"Yes please." She grinned.

"But seriously, you know sex doesn't solve everything?" he asked.

"How do you know me so well?" Tash asked, staring at him.

Nate shrugged. "You wouldn't be the first to try and solve your problems with sex. I tried the sex and drink thing after the car accident but quickly realised that by doing it I was pressing both the pause and the mute button on my life."

Tash blinked hard. It felt like he knew everything about her, that he'd turned her inside out. Or maybe he'd talked to Holly. No, not Holly, she'd never say anything, but maybe Amelia wouldn't be as guarded in sharing Tash's sexual reputation.

Sex had always been a way of getting some affection, however fleeting. There were times in her teens when it was the only affection she received at all. Yes she'd made friends but then they'd moved her on again and she'd had to start over. Until eventually there seemed no point bothering.

They. The suits.

But that's the problem, it's always fleeting, no one ever wants me for keeps. This thing with Nate is amazing but is it really going to last? Really?

She shut her eyes and tried to concentrate on breathing. In and out. In and out. Trying to take the breath down lower.

How would you know they didn't want you for keeps? If you never gave anyone the chance to reject you, that means you never gave anyone a chance to accept you either...

"Anyway, do you want to know...the rest?" She asked brusquely.

"Yes, everything. You seem so sure I'll reject you because of your baggage so tell me what it is and then I'll tell you how we're going to deal with it."

98

He sounded so sure, so confident. How did you get that assurance? The real kind, not the act she'd mastered which had served her pretty well until Nate came along and saw straight through her.

"Okay," she replied, her voice shaky. "I stopped caring, stopped hoping. I didn't just reject people before they rejected me, I rejected the world. I broke whatever the house rules were in my foster placements. I picked fights. By the time I hit thirteen I'd already lost my virginity, knew where I could get drugs and truanted from school."

She glanced at Nate to see how he was taking this. His expression was impassive but his strong fingers still caressed hers, giving her confidence to continue.

"It was when I was thirteen that I started to obsess about my mum's suicide, like I was destined to end up the same. I didn't know how many tablets I needed to take to die so I took lots, I just went into different supermarkets so I could get lots of packets of aspirin without anyone saying anything. I waited until my foster family had gone to bed and then I took them all."

Nate squeezed her hand.

"It turns out that was what saved me." Tash half smiled. "Too many tablets and you vomit them back up. After I threw up I knew I had to try something else. My foster parents locked up anything poisonous so I tried the drain cleaner I'd found in the neighbour's shed. I mixed it with orange juice thinking I'd be able to get it down better but just threw it back up. The orange juice protected my throat from burns apparently. I was *lucky* again but at the time I just felt like it was another thing I couldn't get right. I woke next morning with buzzing in my ears and felt like crap but I was...still alive. Then at school I broke down and told someone and the authorities swooped in and took me off to hospital. My foster mother didn't want me back in the house in case my behaviour affected her *real* kids. They plonked me in an adolescent psychiatric unit for assessment."

She stopped and defiantly scanned Nate's face for any sign of disgust but there was none.

"Go on," Nate squeezed her hand.

Tash sighed. "We had these God-awful group therapy sessions with social workers and doctors. I can still picture my social worker. He had this mangy beard and there always seemed to be bits of food stuck in it. He kept on wanting to talk about sex. I still hate beards even now. Anyway, most of the other patients were either harming themselves in the toilets or taking drugs that'd been smuggled in."

"Was that when you started?" Nate asked, sliding a hand up her arm with the scars.

"Yes." Tash stared down at the floor. "I learnt how to cope in hospital alright but not quite the way they planned. I cut myself or inhaled lighter fuel to blot out pain whenever alcohol and sex couldn't do the job."

"Were you diagnosed with anything?"

"They said there was nothing wrong with me mentally, I was just a...very sad little girl." She gulped, steeling herself not to break down. "I remember the words they used even now. I was supposed to have counselling when I got out but it never got arranged. No one wanted me after the unit so I ended up in a children's home. Then I knew I had to rely on myself. My teen years weren't very happy, it's fair to say."

She laughed, bitterly. "But as I got older I found it easier to process stuff without the need to get off my head or punish my body. When I was eighteen I moved in with a guy just to get a roof over my head. We came to Europe travelling and when we split I stayed. The end. No more baggage to declare."

She sighed, feeling empty but strangely peaceful.

Relieved.

She'd never told anyone the whole lot. She'd let the odd fact slip through her defences but never everything. Not in one go.

"I do understand." Nate kissed her hair. "I understand you got a really shit deal and you did what you needed to protect yourself.

But you've practically turned it into an art form and you don't need it as a defence mechanism any more."

"Why not?" Tash closed her eyes, inhaling Nate's scent again and the faint aroma of wood smoke from the fire.

I'll remember this when he's gone. I can close my eyes and imagine he's next to me.

"Because you're not that little girl anymore, needing someone to look after you. Back then if you'd trusted someone and they let you down it would've been the end of the world, or at least it would have felt like it. But now you're a strong, independent woman." Nate's fingers dipped down over her chest, brushing the curve of her breasts.

She shuddered beneath his fingers, the physical sensations soothing the turbulent emotions. She almost might believe anything Nate said when his lips were on her skin and his low, oh so masculine voice talked her into that wonderful, alternate universe he inhabited where everything was possible.

If only it could be. If only. If only I could have my own happy ending.

"I am?" She nestled against him a small sigh escaping her lips.

"Sure you are." He rested his palm against the flat of her stomach and currents of desire rippled through her from where his fingers curled against her. "Survivors are strong. If you've never had to deal with crap you're not strong, you're simply untested. Now, will you open your eyes?"

"No," Tash replied, shaking her head, still afraid of the pity or disgust she'd surely find in Nate's eyes.

"Please?" Nate's fingers stroked her breasts, stirring the currents of sexual desire, making her nipples ache and strain to meet him through the fabric of her hoodie.

Tash opened her eyes and stared up into Nate's dark blue-grey eyes, searching them intently, feeling the familiar jerk of connection. Familiar, yet always a shock somehow. The connection was so vivid she suddenly understood what the ever-present dull ache in her chest had been - disconnection.

She'd disconnected herself from the world around her, never truly sharing anything of herself, never really letting anyone in, never allowing a sexual fling get to the point where emotional intimacy might follow.

This is what I've been missing. This is what falling in love feels like.

The thought scared her.

He could hurt me, really hurt me. And he doesn't do complications...

"But you don't do complicated," she blurted, unable to bear having sex with him again knowing it might be the last time. She needed...something from him. Nothing big, after all they'd only just met but some indication she actually meant something to him would be enough. Wouldn't it?

I want more. I want to be his girl.

"Maybe I was wrong to say that, to make that choice. It happens. I'm not infallible Tash. I'm just a man. Hard to believe, I know." he grinned.

She snorted and he lightly poked her in the ribs. Then they stared, eyes locked, Nate's pupils darkening in the firelight. The silence in the hut felt intense but starkly honest. Everything had been pared back to what really mattered. There was no place to hide, nowhere to escape to, not in a hurry anyway.

"So, you were saying something about being wrong?" Tash asked.

"It doesn't happen often so I wouldn't be quite so smug if I were you." He laughed but then his expression became more serious. "I just think what's the point of everything I'm trying to do and even the bloody book I'm writing if I don't practice what I preach. That, you know, the crap in people's pasts needn't be insurmountable. That everyone matters."

"Hmm, not the most romantic thing anyone's ever said to me." Tash rolled her eyes.

"What *is* the most romantic thing anyone's said to you?" Nate quirked his lips, edging closer, the gleam in his eyes more than just a reflection of the firelight.

Tash considered. The most unromantic propositions she'd received sprang more readily to mind. There weren't exactly too many romantic moments to choose from.

"Hmm, that would have to be 'You're bloody gorgeous'." She picked the least offensive of the various compliments she'd received.

"You *are* bloody gorgeous." Nate pulled her fully onto his lap.

She could feel his erection beneath her thigh. Her nerve endings fizzed and her body yelled at her to stop talking, to let it take over, because it could manage quite well on its own without any of that stupid thinking stuff, thank you.

But still the niggle buzzed at the back of her mind, like an annoying wasp, trapped in her skull.

You're just one of his projects.

"I need to know that I'm not...not just one of your projects." She turned her face away as he moved in for another kiss. "Madeleine said I was."

"Do you want me to fire Madeleine?" Nate asked, the corners of his lips twitching.

Shall I call his bluff and say yes?

She grimaced. "Seriously Nate, I need to know, am I just going to be a chapter in your book? Your actual book that is, that wasn't supposed to be a crappy metaphor."

"You're not a project Tash, I most definitely don't see you as work. Quite the opposite," Nate said firmly. "I think we have a connection that's special and I want to carry on seeing you after my month at the chalet is up. There are lots of flights between London and Geneva. You shouldn't give a toss what other people say. I don't."

Tash believed him. She imagined he wouldn't care what anyone thought, not even the Prime Minister. He cared about making money to fund his projects, his charities. He really did have integrity. Not to mention a sense of humour and pretty amazing skills in bed.

"Tash?"

"Hmm," she murmured, distracted, nuzzling his neck.

"There isn't an invisible line between my work and myself," Nate said thoughtfully. "My work is what I believe in."

"What? Making money?" Tash snorted again, her lips twitching.

"No smartass, although I am pretty good at that as it happens. Making money is fun."

"Are you going to invest in Scott's business? They're really lovely people." Tash looked up at him imploringly.

"Ah, so that's why you're sleeping with me?" Nate raised an eyebrow and pretended to flinch when she poked him. "Well even though they are nice people I'd never invest because of that."

"Oh, that's a shame." Tash sighed.

"But I will be investing because it's a sound business opportunity. The Swiss franc is rock solid, much safer than the pound or Euro, and with the public investment in Verbier to develop mountain biking tourism it's only going to get better. Plus, I have to say there's a certain...irony in my investing in a business that relieves the super-rich of their cash. After all I'm going to be pumping lots of it into schemes helping the less advantaged. I help to...level things, I suppose you could say."

"You're taking from the rich and giving to the poor." Tash giggled. "You're Robin Effing Hood!"

"I've been called many things but I've never been called that before." Nate laughed and pulled her tighter. His warmth radiated through her body, filling her with a peculiar lightness, as though she might float up to the ceiling of the hut.

"I like it," she said. "Can't see you in green tights though."

Nate laughed and slid one warm hand up the inside of Tash's top, stroking her bare flesh and tweaking her lace covered nipples.

"So you're absolutely sure I'm not a project?" Tash asked, hating herself for being so needy but unable to stop herself asking.

"No," he replied. "Unless you've got a secret business plan tucked away in your knicker drawer?"

"Nope, I don't even have a knicker drawer, just shared floor space under the bunks." She let out a tiny sigh. "I just need to know why...why are you with *me*?"

"Are you fishing for compliments?"

"Of course." She grinned.

"Okay, I'll give you one. I meant it when I said it takes an extra something to survive a crappy childhood and come out an okay person."

"What doesn't kill you makes you stronger you mean?"

"It does, from what I've seen, yes." Nate replied thoughtfully. "Some people do give up. The giving up can take the form of addictions, being institutionalised, signing on with no intention of finding work, oh, all sorts of ways... Or you get over it, leave it in the past and move forward."

"That's what I thought I had done." Tash nestled against Nate, his firm muscle against her slighter frame.

"You did, you just brought a lot of excess baggage with you to Switzerland. But everyone needs a helping hand sometimes."

"Hmm. So, what's the title of your book?" she asked. "Give up or Get Over it'? Or 'Get over it and Get on with it'?"

"Hmm not bad ideas, they could make good chapter headings, but while we're talking about getting on with it..." His hands snaked down inside her leggings to caress her bottom.

"Ahhh... I'm um, still waiting for more compliments," Tash gasped out the words with difficulty, her body almost at tipping point already as his fingers slipped under the lace edge of her knickers and plunged inside her, stroking the wetness up and over her clit.

"You're smart, you're strong and you're funny," Nate said in a low voice, his breath warm against her ear.

"You forgot sexy." She gasped and wriggled against his erection.

He groaned. "I *think* you're sexy but you're going to have to take all your clothes off, just so I can remind myself and make sure."

"Cheeky git," she muttered, yanking her hoodie and vest top

105

over her head.

"Daft mare," he replied, helping her out of her leggings.

He pretended to scrutinise her body in the firelight. "Oh yes. Definitely sexy. You're beautiful Natasha. And you know you're special, right?"

"No one has ever called me special." Tears burned at the back of Tash's eyes but she wouldn't cry. This time she *felt* special. Not just an easy lay or the bolshy girl with the pink hair, nor the girl who grew up in foster care. And she didn't mind him using her full name.

She was Natasha and that was okay.

This wasn't a happy ending because this wasn't an ending, this was a happy beginning.

Beginning to trust.

Beginning to hope.

Beginning to love.

Change isn't always a bad thing.

"Their loss," Nate muttered, pulling his clothes off and sliding his hands over her breasts and then down between her legs.

And then there was no more talking. Just two bodies becoming one by the light of the flickering fire in a tiny mountain hut surrounded by a thick blanket of pristine, powder snow.

More snowflakes fell outside the cabin windows as they lay entwined. Fresh snow created a new blank canvas, covering over the old and making the landscape new again.